BUGGER BANKSY

BY ROY D HACKSAW

Published by Earth Island Books
Pickforde Lodge
Pickforde Lane
Ticehurst
East Sussex
TN5 7BN

www.earthisland.co.uk
© Copyright Earth Island Publishing Ltd 2021

ISBN 978-1-9997581-9-6

Printed, bound and distributed by Ingram Sparks

A NOTE FROM THE AUTHOR

This is obviously a completely made up story about mostly made up people. But on the odd occasion where real life people do appear, they're such over-exaggerated fantasy versions of themselves that they almost certainly won't sue. Probably. And at no point do I ever actually reveal who Bristol's most celebrated mystery artist actually is. In fact, I reckon I've covered most of the half-decent rumours in this little tale, and made up a couple of extra ones just for the hell of it.

This book is dedicated to anyone who's ever had a Banksy slapped on the side of their house, and all the chaos that it brings.

Cheers!

Roy D Hacksaw

FOREWORD

How would you feel if you woke up one morning to find that global guerrilla-graffiti legend Banksy had sprayed one of his artworks on the side of your house? A range of responses seem possible, but chances are you'd be pretty chuffed at having a little slice of the world's most fascinating and enigmatic street artist to call your own.

What then, though? Stop for a second and think about how you'd take to the doorstopping journos and film crews, the endless crowds of hipsters waving their mobile phones at the side of your gaff – the hole blown in the side of your peaceful little life, in short. Mixed blessing, perhaps?

This is the dilemma that faces Glyn and Kevin, the lovably feckless duo at the heart of Roy's tale. When Banksy rocks up at their remote Welsh Valleys farm one autumn night (with a bespoke piece of stencil art that wraps up the troubled recent history of the Valleys in one horribly vivid image), they suddenly find themselves the centre of global art-world attention. Except, in their case, the attention is particularly unwelcome – due to, how shall we put this, a certain creative revenue stream the pair have devised to supplement the modest income of the modern sheep farmer.

Much comedy ensues as the hapless duo attempt to fend off the mounting attention of the south Wales hipsterati (with no help at all from their gossip-hungry local publican); negotiate with a New York modern art power broker; stay on the right side of the local council and their preservation orders; and keep a certain illicit harvest on the move and away from the prying eyes of the local constabulary and 'business' rivals. Oh, and the sheep develop a sudden and very keen interest in this 'harvest' too, with hilarious results.

A remote barn some considerable way up a Welsh valley might seem an odd place for Banksy to place his latest bit of stealth street art. But, as so often with this cunning fella, the place and the message are working in perfect harmony. Glyn's farm sits above a former coal mine ("My old man always used to say that he could hear the miners singing Land Of My Fathers beneath the soil when he was out tending his sheep on a still afternoon" – lovely image, that). Said mine will have been one of the many such to have fallen under Thatcher's axe during the mass pit closures of 1984-85. So, Bugger Banksy's Banksy has come up with the arresting image of the Iron Lady defecating down a mine shaft – an all-too-vivid reminder of how Mrs T royally dumped on South Wales' major employer over three decades ago.

And that is, after all, what elevates Banksy's art above so many of the million chancers and fanboys hoisting themselves up stepladders and daubing their pieces on walls around the world. Many of these works are accomplished enough – but they tend not to have the political bite and sting in the tail of Banksy's, where each piece just works, making its acid little commentary on modern life perfectly in its chosen setting. And as the Banksy of Roy's tale knows perfectly well, a Welsh farmhouse may not seem the most public spot to display your latest piece – but harness the power of Instagram, and you'll have hordes beating a path to your work before you can say 'Where's our livelihood, Maggie?'.

What I most loved about this tale, though, was Roy's affectionate portrayal of a Welsh Valleys community. Thatcher may have decimated the Valleys with her pit and steelworks closures, but Roy's portrait of the valley around the town of Abertillery shows a community getting on with life in myriad inventive, witty ways – from the exotic meats (more seared wildebeest, anyone?) cooked on the George Foreman grill down the local boozer, to the corner shop's vigorous trade in biscuits, cakes and crisps – thanks to the busy local skunk scene and attendant evening munchies. There are some beautiful descriptions of the natural world, too. "The leaves on the trees were just starting to change, too, as the first rich reds and purples and oranges of Autumn began to crack out across the trees at the valley top like some kind of pastoral popcorn." Roy, after penning this, I hope you rewarded yourself with an extra strong cuppa and a raid on the biscuit tin!

Oh, and watch out for the cameo from Roy's punk two-piece. I won't say much more – other than that, when you spot it, you'll be on a roll.

Happy reading, butt!

Steve Wright is arts editor of Bristol24/7 magazine and, previously, of Bristol and Bath's Venue magazine. He is also author of the book Banksy's Bristol: Home Sweet Home, and the editor of Children of the Can: 25 Years of Bristol Graffiti.

1

There are some people who court fame and notoriety. Others that actively avoid it. And there's a third, smaller subset of people who get it thrust upon them entirely against their will, and however hard they might try, they just can't make it go away. You know, like lottery winners, accidental internet sensations, and the people who live next door to murder suspects. Glyn Williams was one such unlucky chap. He'd firmly ticked the non-publicity box of life, and all he really wanted was to be left to himself to quietly go about his business. And of course, when your business is one of the biggest indoor skunk growing operations in the whole of the South Wales Valleys you really do want to keep yourself under the radar.

Of course, his name didn't help. Just after he was born, in the early eighties, Margaret Thatcher deregulated the buses, and a little fella from Ynysddu started up a minibus service that would soon become the biggest coach company in the whole of South Wales. And that little fella just happened to be called Glyn Williams, too. So our Glyn, who was already a shy and reserved lad, grew up seeing his name emblazoned on the sides of buses everywhere he went, and had to endure all his school mates shouting "There's your bus, Glyn! Give us a ride!" every single day of his childhood. Then in later life, when anyone ever asked him his name – teachers, employers, girls in pubs – the response would, without fault, always be something along the lines of: "Oh, like on the side of the buses?" It wasn't his parents' fault, of course. They could never have predicted what was going to happen in the world of transport politics just a few short years after their new arrival's birth. Good solid Welsh name, after all, is Glyn Williams. But given what subsequently transpired, it's no wonder that Glyn soon became something of a recluse. It's also no wonder that he really, really hated Thatcher – and in his case for even more reasons that your standard South Walean could ever begin to imagine.

Glyn lived on his old family farm, up a lane, off another lane, just beyond the Cwmtillery reservoir. His family had been working the land up at Daisy Farm for generations – for almost as long as farmers have been farmers, his old grandpa always used to joke – and he still kept up the front of a traditional farm life, tending sheep on the rolling valley slopes, and growing just enough vegetables to get by without having to pop down to the big Tesco in Abertillery all that often. But out in his old back barn he had an entirely different crop on the go – one that reaped him in a comfortable living with his just-about-manageable list of regular customers, but one that was also never going to trouble the big dealers from down the valley in the bright lights of Cwmbran and Newport.

This cottage industry of Glyn's was perfectly located. Just far enough out of the way and hard to find for there to be no passing traffic or nosy people sticking their beaks into his business, but still close enough to the big smoker's haunts of Blaina and Brynmawr and Garndiffaith to give him a small but trustworthy income stream. Folk kept themselves to themselves around these parts, and the quietly efficient black economy that began to build itself into a viable alternative to big business around the time of the miners' strike meant that everybody – well, nearly everybody – turned a blind eye to many of the more quietly nefarious goings on in the darker creases of the local farm lanes.

The biggest problem that Glyn had in keeping his lucrative side hustle under the radar came in the winter. This corner of the Valleys was a fair bit above sea level. So even when the inhabitants of the big cities down by the coast were only just beginning to think about getting their big coats out, up at the top of the valley the hoar frosts would bite in hard, or the snow would begin to settle. If that happened, the roof on the barn at Daisy Farm would stand out like a dark beacon among the sea of white that surrounded it, the snow and ice all melted by the heat of the lamps needed to keep his pungent merchandise safely warm all year round. At first he tried a heath robinson kind of cooling mechanism to keep the roof space cool, using warm air blowers and the pipes from his late Nan's old Henry vacuum cleaner. But that proved to be too noisy, as on a cold still night you could pretty much hear it from three valleys away. So then Glyn and his mate Kevin came up with the bright idea of painting the barn's rooftop with that crusty fake snow spray stuff that you get at Christmas. You know, to fill in the corners of your front windows and make it look all festive. It might have looked a bit rubbish up close, but from across the valley – and more importantly, from the window of a police helicopter – it looked like any other frosty rooftop. And what's more, if you bought the cheap stuff it would wash away with the first rains that would always inevitably follow the snows.

Life was pretty good for Glyn Williams. He didn't get up to all that much, but it was quiet. It was calm. And it just kept ticking along nicely. That is until one night when a little fella from across the bridge toddled along and whupped his life into a proper unexpected turmoil.

2

It was a still, warm night in the middle of September, right at the end of a long old dry spell. The colour was just beginning to change on the mountains across the valley. The dusty dry brown that had seemed to have been around for an age now was slowly being edged out by the first few nervous patches of green that anyone had seen in months, encouraged to emerge from the scorched earth by the first few heavy dews of the season. The leaves on the trees were just starting to change, too, as the first rich reds and purples and oranges of Autumn began to crack out across the trees at the valley top like some kind of pastoral popcorn.

Glyn had Kevin round to catch up on a few old Jet Li DVDs and have a nice quiet smoke and a cup of tea. He'd brought a big bag of cans round, too, and the pair were just beginning to get pretty nicely relaxed. But about 20 minutes into their third film of the night, Kung Fu Cult Master, Glyn suddenly thought that he could hear an unfamiliar noise coming from outside. Obviously, considering both the remote location, AND the clandestine nature of his little business operation, he was instantly suspicious, and more than a little bit concerned. Unexpected noises of an obviously human nature generally only led to complications, be they the police, the press, the drug lords of Cwmbran, or just unwitting nosy parkers who could stumble across their stash and put the word out. Or worst of all, crusty bus dwellers looking for somewhere quiet to park up. "Good, honest, well-intentioned folks," Kevin always reasoned, but a people with a curious cosmic telepathy for a nice quiet parking spot well away from the prying eyes of the authorities. And as soon as they find one it's almost as if they call across the valleys by moonlight like slightly niffy dreadlocked wolves, attracting more and more of their kind as they howl into the darkness. And to be fair, that's the last thing Glyn needed, however good for custom it might be in the short term.

"What was that, Kevin butt?" Glyn quietly clucked, perking his head up on an angle like a household dog who thinks they just heard something unusual in the distance. "Whassat Glyn mate? I didn't hear anything?" Kevin replied, his eyes not quite sitting in their standard configuration at this point. "There it is again," Glyn whispered, now leaning towards the door with a more urgent expression on his face. "It sounds like someone moving a metal step ladder about. I hope it's not them totters nicking slates off the barn roof again. It took bloody ages to match up the new ones after the last time!" He quickly hit mute on the TV's controller, right at the point where Zhang Wuji was about to fall off the cliff. "Ohhh dammit, Glyn, this is my favourite bit!" moaned Kevin. "Shhhh!" Glyn spat back, "Bloody listen man!"

"Ohhhh, I hear it now," said Kevin, his head fast clearing with the possible urgency of the situation.

"It's not them rozzers putting up a spy cam, is it?"

Kevin was famed for his paranoia about the police. For years he thought his Mam was an informant for the local Heddlu, just because he kept seeing her chatting to the local beat bobby PC Alan and passing him suspicious looking packages. Turned out that they were distant cousins, and she used to supply the policeman's missus with eggs from her coop out back. It still took him years to entirely trust her again, even though in actual fact she'd done absolutely nothing wrong. But this time he might just have had a point. After all, Glyn's little business had been ticking along nicely for a couple of years now, and they had to get found out some time, surely. Glyn's skunk was a pretty rich crop mind, so it was hardly surprising that Kevin was often prone to joining in the dots where there were no dots at all. Or paper, for that matter.

"Ohhhh shut up Kev, you paranoid knob, it's not the bizzies. But there is definitely someone out there rattling about. Let's go round the back way and catch them in the act. I don't want them putting bloody big holes in that roof again. That was too much bloody hassle before. Tool up, butt. Tool up."

Of course, neither Glyn or Kevin were in any fit state to trouble anyone, let alone scare away any marauding roof tile thieves. Them boys from down the Valley were notorious for nicking anything if it stopped moving for more than five minutes. During the scrap metal boom a few years back there wasn't a single manhole cover or garden gate left anywhere from Nantyglo to Crumlin. Everyone's dogs were getting stuck down drains like some weird canine suicide pact. But these petty thieves always carried pretty heavy and pointy equipment with them, so it was always better to approach them armed, just in case, like. Glyn picked up a big old pitchfork that had been leaning against the outhouse for some years now, while Kevin grabbed a ladle from the kitchen, and one of those big super squirter water pistols that Glyn kept in the house to keep the cats away from the barn. He always dropped a few spoonfuls of ground chilli seeds in with the water just to deter the scraggy moggies from shitting in his prize troughs. To this day he had no idea quite where the cats actually came from, as no one lived within at least a mile of Daisy Farm, but they were still a right pain in the arse, wherever they lived.

The hapless pair skulked out of the kitchen door, quietly stalking their prey. "What have you got that poxy ladle for, butty?" Glyn power-whispered incredulously to his mate.

"Well Glyn, I thought that if things got tense I could just bonk them on the head with it," Kevin blustered back. "And to be fair, it was the first thing that came to hand when I swung my arms about aimlessly about in the kitchen. Well, you made me rush now, isn't it."

"Prat!" Glyn replied, before jutting out an arm to halt Kevin in his blundering tracks.

"There he is, the little arsebag. But what's he bloody doing?" Glyn rasped, as a smell reminiscent of pear drops filled the air and a gentle hissing sound crept through the night.

"Looks like he's painting something on the side of your old dad's barn, Glyn," Kevin replied.

"You're bloody right an' all. Some cheeky bleeder's graffing us up, out here, in the middle of bloody nowhere! And that's just not polite! Right, I'm going up there to chase the daft bastard off. Stick with me, Kev!"

The pair paced slowly towards the hooded figure, like cats creeping after a moving leaf. But the figure was so embroiled in the reverie of his artistic creation that he didn't notice the two men until they were almost at the foot of his fold-up ladder.

"Oi! Banksy! What the bloody hell do you think you're doing tagging up my barn? Piss right off, and take all your tins and shit with you, now!" Glyn shouted angrily at the dark human shape that was spraying on his wall.

The hooded figure looked up with a start, catching himself off balance and nearly falling from the ladder into the dark lane below. He looked startled, and began to stutter out an explanation in a soft Bristolian accent, his Rs rolling like a cheese down a Gloucestershire hillside. "Erm, erm, sorry gents. I didn't mean to disturb you. I thought this barn was deserted..." he anxiously stuttered.

Kevin butted in to the dark figure's wobbling flow. "Well it's not, you mutt. Now why don't you just piss off back over the bridge where you belong before I ladle you!"

All three men stopped and looked a bit bewildered at this most uncommon threat for a total of around three seconds, before the man on the ladder continued. "It's all part of my wider body of work about the cultural mores of Britain..." he blustered out.
"Let me stop you there, sunshine!" Glyn asserted. "I'm not having you..."

Kevin interrupted his friend: "Cultural what did he say?"

"Dunno Kev. He's one of those poncey art student types from over the Bristol Channel who's up around these parts here doing a bit of misery tourism, innit."

"I see," replied Kevin. "I think..."
"Anyway mate, you ain't bloody National Geographic. You're dirtying up my barn with your shitty tags. Now piss off back over the bridge like a good boy and get back to that posh flat yer

Mam's paying for before you get a taste of my pitchfork!" Glyn threatened in an over dramatic voice, before halfheartedly waving his pointy weapon at the figure. The man on the ladder was now looking more than a little concerned for his safety. By reflex he jolted back at Glyn's first jab of the pitchfork, and his hood fell down a little. Through the gloom Glyn could just about pick out that this was no young student type by any means, but instead a middle-aged man with round glasses and a fairly worried expression on his face.

"Shit, look at you pops!," Glyn barked, incredulously. "You're older than me! You're way too long in the tooth to be doing any of this adolescent vandalism stuff. Take a look at yourself. Bloody grow up, butt!"

He jostled his pitchfork a bit more angrily now, but still the figure on the ladder tried to explain what he was doing and why he was here.

"Whoa, there! Calm down now, erm, Glyn, is it? This doesn't have to end in violence. That's always a bad option. This painting that I'm doing is a social commentary on how Thatcher's England tried to destroy the industry, and indeed the culture, of South Wales…"

"OK then Picasso," Glyn shouted sarcastically, "Why are you doing all this on the side of my barn and not in some posh art gallery down in Cardiff?"

"Well Glyn," the man on the ladder explained, "I wanted to find somewhere that was actually directly above a mine to leave my mark, and all the old pit buildings that are left scattered around

The Valleys are already covered in tags. So this was the only decent-sized wall that I could find that was not only clean enough to paint on, but that was almost certainly located over a mine tunnel. It is over a mine isn't it?"

"Damn right, butty. My old man always used to say that he could hear the miners singing Land Of My Fathers beneath the soil when he was out tending his sheep on a still afternoon. But I just thought that he'd been sniffing the sheep dip again and never entirely believed him. But there's definitely mining tunnels running under our feet all around here, so you're probably right," Glyn explained calmly, before he realised his anger had been quelled a little and he was beginning to lose his confrontational mojo. A generally quiet man, if perhaps a little grumbly, Glyn hardly ever lost his temper at all, and so wanted to make the most of the situation while his blood was up. "But that's beside the point, you ageing vandal knob. I want you off that ladder, and off that wall, and fucking the fuck off back to wherever you bloody came from before I count to ten. And yes, before you ask, I actually CAN count to ten!"

"But.. but…" the now uncowled figure sputtered. "Just give me ten minutes to finish this off and it could make you millions!"
"I'll finish you off," piped up Kevin, out of nowhere, and he pumped the super squirter up, hit the trigger and got a powerful stream of chilli-infused water right in the mystery tagger's eyes.

"Owww! Owwwwwww! That bloody stings! What have you put in that bloody water, you idiot?" the figure yelled out, appearing to be in some considerable discomfort.

"The finest Dorset Naga chilli seeds," Glyn interjected. We grow them out back, then grind them up and put them in the water pistol to keep the cats off the crops. And there's plenty more where that came from. So on your way, prick."

The now panicking graffiti man quickly slid down his ladder, before stopping to pick up his dropped cans and tear his stencil from the wall, all the while blinking hard at the flaming terror that was now beginning to eat its way into his eyes. He pulled down his ladder, stuffed it under his arm and scuttled off to his dark coloured estate car, hidden away in a passing place about thirty yards up the lane, accidentally scattering the odd little bit and piece of his equipment as he went.
"You'll be sorry," the figure shouted with pain in his voice. "No, you really will be sorry when you find out..."

"Find out what? The only sorry thing around here is you, you sorry streak of sorry piss overgrown schoolboy grandad tagging knob!" Kevin bleated, somewhat incoherently. The figure jumped in his car and sped off down the lane, before realising all too soon that the direction he had driven in only led to some empty farm buildings and a big metal gate. So rather awkwardly he had to carry out a panicked twelve-point-turn before embarrassingly having to drive towards Daisy Farm again with with his tail between his legs.

"I thought he'd soon realise he couldn't get out that way, Glyn," chortled Kevin. "Shall I squirt him again?"

"Yeah, go on Kev. Just to let him know that we saw him being a useless bastard in the car. You're not usually that good an aim with the cats, mun," Glyn added, somewhat startled at his pal's new found shooting prowess.

"I think it was all the excitement, Glyn," replied Kevin. "I'm an anxious man, as you know. But somehow, when it really comes to the crunch, I seem to get a clear mind and everything comes into focus. I really think that I ought to become a snooker referee!"

"You what, you random git?" Glyn questioned his pal with a bewildered look on his face. "Oh wait, here he comes again. Squirt the little toerag one more time, just so that he remembers not to come back around this way in a hurry."

Kevin drew back the pump action bit of his trusty weapon and began to squirt. Somehow he managed to get the stream of stinging water right through the tiny crack in the top of the window and soak the driver within.

"You squirting philistine fools!" the figure in the car shouted angrily as he sped off into the distance, the glow of his red tail lights disappearing off into the dark like an angry baboon.

"Well that was a very strange to do, Kevin," Glyn remarked. "I wonder what all that was about?
Anyway, we'll clear all that mess up tomorrow when it's light. Let's get back in and watch the end of the film."

"Ohhhh no man, you've got to rewind to the cliff bit. I bloody love the cliff bit," Kevin enthusiastically cried.

"And I'll tell you what, Kev," Glyn added. "You weren't wrong about the calm-under-pressure bit. I'll have a look on the websites for the snooker people tomorrow and see if they've got any referee training schemes going. Although you'd probably have to lay off the draw for a bit or you'd start getting scared of the balls and thinking that anyone in the crowd with a cough was trying to get you."

"Good point, Glyn," replied Kevin, "I clearly didn't think that through. I might knock that idea on the head. There must be some kind of professional role that involves remaining calm under pressure while also remaining a sketchy pot head. I'll have a big think about it."

"Brew, Kevin?"

"That'll be lovely, ta, Glyn. Got any biscuits?"

"Only them own-brand Rich Tea from the Co-Op?"

"They'll do, Glyn. They'll do..."

3

Glyn and Kevin had known each other since before they could remember. Both men were an only child, so kind of bonded together like brothers at pre-school playgroup. They were only eight months apart, age wise, although in different years at school, so Glyn reluctantly accepted the role of the wise, if not slightly aloof older brother figure, while Kevin was the more annoying-yet-stillloveable younger sibling type. They were actually related, vaguely, but in that way that simple language can't easily explain. Their mums were cousins, or half-cousins or three steps removed or something like that, although no one could ever quite work out the official familial term for it. But somewhere down the line they had a common blood relative, and that was good enough for them to refer to themselves as cousins, even if strictly speaking they almost certainly weren't. Probably.

They'd both had their share of family sadness, too. Glyn's Mam died on his seventh birthday. He was never entirely sure of what, because he was too young to fully grasp it when it happened, and his old man never really wanted to talk about it after he'd grown up a bit and developed a questioning mind. But he remembered her being really fragile for a long time before she went, and she was never quite able to have the kind of boisterous fun and games that all the other Mams seemed to relish. As the years have gone on his few living memories of his Mam have begun to fade, instead reduced to peering out of the windows of the handful of photographs that his dad kept, with his frail and stick-like Mother smiling bravely through the pain at some Christmas or birthday gathering or another.

His dad never really got over it either, confining himself to the farm for months on end and walking the sheep all over the mountain for days at a time. So Glyn had a quiet and lonely sort of upbringing, reading piles of comics, or watching Hammer horror films and endless martial arts epics until way after the standard bedtime for a lad of his age. And then when Kevin started coming up more often they'd go off into the woods on epic adventures, building camps and digging massively deep holes just because they could.

Sometimes Glyn's dad would take them both on long walks through the countryside, teaching them how to recognise deer tracks and badger runs, and helping them to learn the songs of every kind of bird life that ever passed their way. They were the best times with Glyn's old man. They didn't happen all that often, but when they did they were like priceless jewels that the two boys cherished forever. They'll never forget that time they saw that stark white albino buzzard getting bombed and mobbed by all the other birds – probably just for being different and standing out a bit from the other wildlife. The two boys watched it and watched it until it passed over the hilltop, still pursued by the crows and the starlings and the magpies. They felt a bit of a kinship with that poor old bird. A couple of lads who didn't quite fit in with the crowd, but who kept themselves to themselves and wandered around the mountain, learning stuff as they went.

Glyn's dad was always a bit of a strange beast, emotionally. He could go for weeks and weeks barely talking, with a cold, stone-faced demeanour. But then every now and again he'd hit a really low patch, and there was no consoling him for what seemed like ages. He'd always been prone to bouts of depression after Glyn's Mam died, but it always seemed to come on worse after he'd been dipping the sheep. Glyn's dad was a hands-on sort of a farmer, and used to get right in amongst it when it was dipping time. So all the farmers up the valley feared that he was suffering from a longterm dose of organophosphate poisoning that he'd accumulated from some of the chemicals in the dip, which had long been suspected to cause depressive episodes among sheep farmers. His dark spells got worse and worse, and it finally came to a head during that foot and mouth outbreak back in 2001. DEFRA, or whatever it was called back then, hadn't got this far up the valley with their testing squads yet, so he drove all his stock out across the hills and onto the old rugby pitch at Talywain to keep them out of harm's way until the worry had passed. But someone in the village shopped him to the police and had all his stock slaughtered. That was a bridge too far for the poor old sod, and so he took to his shed and glugged down a half pint of sheep dip – a sadly common way for farming types to top themselves back in those days. But strangely, after so many years of working closely with the stuff he seemed to be partially immune to its intricate poisons. So he went and grabbed his rabbit gun and saw himself off more messily in the back shed.

Thankfully it wasn't the by-then late teenaged Glyn who found him, but one of the lads who used to come round and help him maintain the farm machinery. But from this day on Glyn has had a vivid mental picture of what his old man must have gone through in those final minutes, and he too has never been quite the same since. The local farming community were great though, and when DEFRA finally gave the all clear they each donated a handful of sheep to Glyn to help him build up his stock and continue the family farming trade. They were a bit of a nuisance at first, those darned sheep, but he had learned well at the hands of his dad, and took to the farming life much more easily than he'd expected. Unsurprisingly though he vowed to keep things strictly organic, and removed every last trace of sheep dip from the farm.

Kevin's childhood wasn't perhaps as tragic as Glyn's, but it still shaped him in a very major way. His Mam and dad were never truly a couple in the traditional sense of the word, as his old man was always off for months on end, doing who knows what, while his Mam stayed home and dutifully kept the household going. He's got only sketchy memories of his father. He remembers a big, loud, exciting man with massive hands who always smelled of engine oil and cheap cigarettes. On the few occasions that he did grace the family with an all too brief visit, he'd return with presents and promises and half an eye on the door. Then one night, when Kevin was about eleven, he left for the final time, and Kevin has never seen from that day since.

It was always the family myth that he'd run away with the circus, but it was a myth that actually turned out to be true. He started his working life jobbing with the fairgrounds, which is where he met Kevin's mum. He'd tried to settle down a number of times, but the staid family life just wasn't for him, and so when he got offered a slot as a mechanic for one of those cheap old circuses that used to work their way around Wales, he jumped at the chance, and hightailed it off to soak up the glamour of seaside places like Barry Island, Aberystwyth and Rhyl. Kevin only knew this because he'd get the occasional postcard now and again, or if he was lucky, a little parcel with a stick of rock in and an invite to come and see him on the coast some time. But as much as he begged his Mam to let him go and visit him she was never entirely keen, and after a couple of years, even the postcards dried up.

But despite all of this sadness and tragedy, Glyn and Kevin just got on with life, and became terrifically close pals. They each, of course, had their lonely times, but they were as family as family could get without actually being related – well, more than the vague wisp of blood that they possibly shared between them. And it was tough to earn a living in The Valleys just after the turn of the century. Many of the small towns and villages had still yet to recover from the cultural devastation of Thatcher's pit and industry closures, and it was well before all that EU money started trickling in to help the area with regeneration. So Glyn got Kevin to help him with the sheep and with his vegetables, and the pair lived an almost self-sufficient lifestyle for a while, despite both being as poor as church mice for longer than they cared to remember.

They'd started up their alternative business almost by accident. They'd been casual smokers since their early teens, but the quiet lads that they were they'd never really liked the idea of going to see some heavy in Cwmbran to get their herb. So they sent away to America to buy some seeds, entirely for personal use, mind, and it just kind of built from there into the quietly successful little fringe business that it was today. Now you have to remember that there's a lot of this kind of thing going on up around that way, and it's not as frowned upon as perhaps it would be further down the mountain. The Valleys were pretty much abandoned and left to fend for themselves for a good couple of decades after the Thatcher years, and so they developed an alternative economy all of their own. They might only be a short three-hour drive from London, but they might as well have been in the Outer Hebrides for all the powers that be in London cared. And so left to their own devices, they made their own entertainment.

You also have to remember that back then there was pretty much piss all to do around those parts. The Miner's Institutes were all starting to close down, and many of the towns and villages around their way were beginning to resemble a real life St Fagans, as so many of the shops and pubs had shut that all you could really do was wander around and gawp at the attractive brickwork as if you were in a real life living museum.

This in turn resulted in huge groups of bored scallies hanging around under street lights in knock off sportswear causing noise and general antisocial unrest, so the local constabulary were often willing to turn a blind eye to the localised production of skunk, just as long as it didn't turn into too much of a major gang-led industry. Because if it could keep the bulk of the populace subdued and at home, that was one less disorder possibility for them to worry about. And if that wasn't enough, it helped keep the local cornershops in business, too, as the knock-on effect of the skunk trade led to a steep increase in the sales of cakes and crisps and biscuits of an evening.

So while Glyn and Kevin were fairly sure that the local boys in blue had an idea of what they were up to, they never actually asked any of them about it, just to keep on the safe side. After all, pretty much all of their trade went to local smokers and families who just wanted to buy one plant for the garden, or maybe a packet of seeds to try growing themselves. What they did with them from that point on was their own business. Their old barn might make them fifty to eighty grand in a good year, but that almost wasn't the point of it. They had no plans to expand into a more seriously industrial scale, and they were quite happy to just calmly plod along at their own pace, supplying their friends and family while keeping well away from the heavier end of the local drugs trade.

But as you now know, things were about to get a little bit more complicated for them…

4

It was the morning after their unexpected visitation. Glyn and Kevin both woke up on their respective sofas with the menu screen of Kung Fu Cult Master chugging away in the background, and Rich Tea crumbs scattered untidily down the front of both of their t-shirts.

"Ohhhhh, that was a funny old night, Glyn. I had a dream that some Bristol herbert came along and painted up your barn," slurred Kevin, his mouth still sticky with early morning gloop.

"Ha!" proclaimed Glyn with a chuckle on his voice, before an "Ohhh?" and a "Wait a minute!" followed in short order. "That did actually happen, didn't it! Oh man, let's get out there and have a look at what rubbish he's left us to clear up, the dirty shitbag".

The pair shuffled out of the front door, tottering around to the barn's gable end with their feet only half-stuffed in to their battered trainers. As they got through the empty gate and down onto the road they began to see the mess that their artistic invader had left behind.

"Oh man, look at the dirty bastard! He's dropped all sorts of rubbish down the lane," drawled Kevin.

"Well, he was in a bit of a hurry with you and your super squirter gushing red hot fluid at his chubby little face. It's hardly surprising he dropped half of what he was carrying in the dark, what with you chasing after him all guns blazing and that!" Glyn laughed. "Let's have a look at what he's left behind, Kev."

The two men could see a terrible mess left scattered down the lane. A handful of spray cans, with their lids askew, a couple of rolls of masking tape – and somewhat unexpectedly a plastic Tupperware box full of sandwiches that had spewed its load out onto the gravel. And in the middle of it all was a scrunched up bundle of cardboard, sprayed with paint on a few small corners.

"What in the name of heck is that dollop of screwed up nonsense, Kevin?" asked Glyn, curiously.

"I reckon that's the bastard's stencil, Glyn?" Kevin replied?

"Stencil?" Glyn asked, a little confused. "Don't they just spray shit up and see what happens?"

"Nah Glyn. A lot of these poncey art blokes these days knock up a couple of cardboard stencils of what they want to paint, and then just hit and run at their designated location when they reckon they've found the right place for it," Kevin explained.

"The lazy squirt bags," Glyn bellowed, incredulously. "They can't even be bothered to get up there and craft a design like we did in our days, Kev? That's even more bloody cheeky!"

"These are different times, Glyn. Different times indeed," Kevin replied. "And anyway, the most artful thing you ever painted up was 'Kev sucks sheep' in shiny gold biro in that bus shelter by Abergavenny Town Hall when you were twelve, Glyn. That's hardly high art, innit"

"Ohhh, you know what I mean, Kev. This stencil business, it's almost like cheating."

They walked towards the pile of crumpled card and flattened it out it to try to work out what it portrayed.

"Whassat then, Kev? I can't quite work out what it is?"
"I dunno, Glyn. I can see the shape of a face, but it's all backwards. Let's hold it up to the sky and see if it looks any different."

Glyn was surprised by his old pal's sudden display of practical nous, but he thought better of calling it up. It might not happen again after all, so he wanted to cherish the moment. Both men grabbed a corner by the white masking tape and held it aloft to the clouds.

"Ohhhh fucking hell," proclaimed Glyn, anxiously, "that's fucking Thatcher! And she's sitting on the bog! Bloody bleeding typical that is!"

"Hang about Glyn,' Kev cut in, "That looks like it's the old pithead from Glyn Pits that she's sat on. And what's that she's curling off down the mine? Is that coal or is it money?"

"I can't quite tell from here Kev. I reckon we'd have to know what colour paint that bozo was using. And anyway…"

Glyn suddenly froze mid stream, his eyes blazing in abject horror.

"Awwww fuck, mun. So what's that speccy tool actually painted on the side of my barn, then?" he muttered with some concern on his breath.

Both men turned, slowly, then gasped at what confronted them.

"That horrible little bastard has only gone and painted Thatcher having a shit on the side of my bloody barn, hasn't he now!" Glyn shouted in dismay. "Of all the bloody people in the whole damn bloody world it had to be that old witch. And what's worse, he's only done her head and arse and a few other bits, so now I've got to look at her shit-face every time I walk up the lane. We've got to get the wire brush and turps out, mate!"

Glyn was right. The mystery night caller has painted our once inglorious leader in full Spitting Image mode, her beak-like nose hooking out across the wall, and the tendons in her neck all stretched out like a rutting tortoise on the job. She was squatted down with her stately undertrollies around her ankles – and that was it. None of the other more artistic clever stuff from lower down on the stencil. Just the most hated woman in the history of the valleys taking a dump in giant size on the side of Glyn's old barn. You could quite understand his pain.

"Right, let's go and dump all this lot in the wheelie skip down the lane and put the breakfast on," Kevin chirped up. "We've got plenty of time to get rid of that old crone on the wall. Toast, Glyn?"

"Ohhhh, I'd love a couple of slices of toast, Kev!" Glyn enthused. "We still got any of that squidgy white bread with the bits in it? I love that stuff!"

"I'll have a look, Glyn," said Kevin. "There must be some left kicking about by the bread bin. Marmite Glyn?"

"Oh yes please. I love the smell of Marmite in the morning, I does."

5

Glyn and Kevin pondered the strange events of the night before over their toast.

"Who do you think that was last night?" asked Glyn. "Do you think it really was that Banksy? It looks a bit like all that stuff he does. But why the heck would he be up round here?"

"I dunno, Glyn," Kevin replied. "But it does feel a little bit legit – despite it being a great big picture of Thatcher looking like she's giving birth to a coalmine. It's kind of got his germs on it"

"I don't reckon it was him though," Glyn added. "I heard it that it was that bloke out of that miserable band from Bristol, anyway. What is it, Massive Attack? That old bastard definitely didn't look like him!"

"What, that 3G bloke?" asked Kevin.

"Not 3G, you tool, 3D!" barked Glyn with a smile at the corner of his mouth. "3G is one of those plastic football pitches, innit."

"Oh yeah, 3D," Kevin replied, sheepishly. "Anyway, I'm pretty sure that it's not him. I met him at a warehouse party over in Bristol back in the early 90s and he was a right miserable bastard. I can't begin to believe that he's anywhere near as funny, or as clever, as all those Banksy pictures suggest he is. AND he tried copping off with my missus of the time when I was stood right next to them both. Nah, I can't believe it was him."

"Hang about," Glyn asked, with a puzzled look on his face, "Are you sure that it was actually matey bollocks from Massive Attack who tried to have a go on your old missus? I seem to remember that you were in a permanent whooshy haze back then. It could have been any old haunted-looking poser in an expensive coat."

"Yeah, I'm pretty sure it was him…" Kevin replied, with a look on his face like he was delving deeply into the dusty mental Rolodex of his memory. "He looked a bit like that ghostly face you always used to see in the end credits of Star Trek, but you never ever saw the episode it came from, and just assumed that it was some kind of in-joke from the crew. You know the one I mean?"

"What in the name of curtains are you blathering on about now, Kev?," Glyn mocked. "But yes, I know the character to which you refer."

"Well kind of like a cross between him and a taller version of kd laing. It had to be him."

"I'm still not convinced, Kev. I'm still not convinced," replied Glyn, knowingly shaking his head in a manner that suggested he had this kind of conversation with Kevin on pretty much a daily basis.

"And anyway, Glyn added, quickly steering the subject elsewhere. "I also heard that it wasn't one person at all, but bloody loads of them. There may have been an original dabber called Banksy, back in the day. But now the lazy git has just got a few factories full of indentured workers in a dozen different countries that pump out the old shite he plasters on all them poor sods' walls. Then if anyone gets caught brush-handed when they're up a ladder they can all start shouting "I'm Spartacus! No, I'm Spartacus" until nobody knows what's what any more. Plus, it means the sly old bastard can get away with selling more

25

mugs and t-shirts off the back of other people's hard work. Actually, the more I think about it, the more it sounds like a pretty decent business model to me."

Glyn stopped for a moment and looked quizzically into the middle distance. "Just imagine that though. If you did get a proper Banksy slapped on the side of your house," he pondered. "Imagine how many shades of a nightmare that could prove to be. Thank Christ that wasn't actually him."

At the same time that Glyn was off on one of his signature rants, Kevin had half turned off and was checking through his social media. He'd had a quick cycle though Twitter and Facebook, but nothing much had popped up of any particular interest, apart from the usual funny otter videos and Flat Earther conspiracy theories that he was fascinated by. But it was only when he flicked onto Instagram that he sat bolt upright in shock and surprise, like someone had slapped him around the head with a brick tennis racket covered in Spam.

"Errrrm Glyn mate. Stop talking for a minute, would you," Kevin uttered, slowly, with all the fear of the ancients written across his pasty face. "You really need to take a look at this…"

"What is it now, you great galumphing nit?," Glyn proclaimed with his best patronising voice on. "It's not another labrador jumping into big piles of leaves, is it? Or some more of that sheeple shit, eh? Give us the phone here a minute…"

Glyn wrenched the smeary and well-out-of-date smartphone from Kevin's hands and begun to peer through the cracked screen to find out what Kevin had been getting so agitated about. As his eyes finally made sense of what he could just about make out though the jigsaw of broken glass they instantly widened to the size of his Nan's old saucers. "Fuuuuuuuuuuuk…."

6

Glyn blinked hard. Twice. But he still couldn't believe his actual eyes. For there it was, in tiny squares, right in front of him. Banksy's Insta with a handful of photographs of that incomplete Thatcher portrait that was stinking up the old barn's gable end.

"That cheeky old sod must have come back this way to take some photographs after we'd passed out, Glyn," said Kevin. "You've got to admire the nerve of the man after everything we put him through, mind."

"This has got to be fake though, right?" Glyn asked with a worried tone in his voice. "There's no way he's got a standard social media account is there? I mean, it's hardly secret now, is it! Check his Arsebook to see if it's up there too?"

"Nah Glyn, he's not got one," Kevin replied, strangely knowingly. "He famously doesn't have one. He only uses the Instagram and his own website to announce stuff to the world, and the Insta is usually first."

"How do we know this is him though, Kev? It could be anyone, surely?

"Look for the blue tick by his name. If that's there, it's mos deffo him."

"Ohhhhhh bollocks, there is. A blue tick. Shit," Glyn answered. "At least he doesn't say where we are, does he? What does this say under here?"

"Click on it, mate, that'll expand it and you can read the whole thing," Kevin suggested.

"Ohhh, alright then…"

Glyn clicked where it said 'more' and the pair leaned in to read the tiny screen.
"So I got caught last night. Up in the Welsh Valleys. I thought the place was empty, but the owners chased me off with actual pitchforks. Although I'm kinda glad, because thinking about it, it wasn't one of my better works. Sorry Glynn and Kev – you can sell off my stencil and collect a few bob to make up for it, and to help tidy up your wall."

"Ohhhhhh bollocks,' Glyn intoned, with even more panic in his voice than before. It really is him. How the hairy fuck did he know our names, Kevin?"

"Everyone does, Glyn," Kevin chipped up, "All we bloody do is call each other by our names all the bloody time. We'd be terrible bankrobbers, mind. The old bill would be waiting around our house before we got home."

"You know what this means though, Kevin?" Glyn asked, before heading off on a brief sideways tangent. "…awww damn, you're right butty – that bloody name thing. We've got to stop doing that! Anyway, you know what this means? This place is going to turn into a bloody circus as soon as anyone recognises our names. We're bloody done for. We've got to scrape that bastard thing off, quick smart."

No sooner as the words had left his lips, Glyn's phone rang.

"Shit, who's that? It could be anyone?," stressed Glyn in a slightly paranoid tone at the unrecognised number. "They're after us already!"

"Nah mate, it's probably just some call centre from The Philippines trying to sell you something you don't really want while they're ripping off your card numbers," Kevin suggested.

"No, no," said Glyn with panic on his breath, "It's a local number. An actual phone phone. Should I answer it?"

"Yeah man," chimed Kevin. "It'll only be a customer or summat whose got a new number. No cause for concern."
"Yeah, you're right. I'm getting paranoid. I'll answer it…"

Glyn tapped on the big green dot and anxiously began to listen.

"Is that Glyn? Glyn Williams?" the voice enquired. "It's Bob from the Green Dragon pub down in Abertillery. We hear you've got a Banksy. Is it OK if me and the missus come up and have a gander, like. We'll keep it to ourselves, mind."

Bob was one of those barmen who in plain actual fact, kept nothing to himself. Not a bloody sausage. If he got a wind of something that might have been going on, then half the valley would know by teatime, and this was exactly the kind of thing that Glyn and Kevin didn't want getting out. Glyn had to quickly think on his feet.

"Whassat Bob?" he responded. "Noooo mun, are you joking? We wouldn't be so bloody lucky. It must be on the side of some other fortunate bastard's shed."

"Well, it looks a lot like the side of your old barn, Glyn," Bob countered. "And when we saw your names on that Banksy's Instagram account we thought it had to be you?"

"Not us, butt," Glyn mistruthed, half-convincingly. "There's got to be a hundred other Glyns and Kevs across all the valleys. Look, it's even a different spelling on my name and all! Two Ns there, see, not one."

"Ohhhhh, good point Glyn," said Bob, now seeming to stray from the scent a little. "Shall I come up anyway for a cup of tea and a chatter and a smoke? Just me, mind, not Elaine. You know she frowns on me doing that kind of larky these days"

"Nah mate, that's alright. The next crop's not going to be ready for a few weeks anyway. I'll give you a shout when it's all fully grown."

Glyn was fairly sure that he'd got Bob off his case, but thought he'd add a little extra, just to be more convincing, like.
"And if you do happen to find out where that Banksy is, give us a shout, mate. We'd love to go and have a look at it ourselves, me and Kev, and we know how you keep your ear to the ground! I've never seen one in real life before."

"Fair do's," Bob replied. "We'll keep our eyes and ears peeled. And while I'm here, butt, you coming down to our indoor barbecue next Sunday? We're getting a whole load of exotic meats in?"

"Indoor barbecue?" Glyn enquired, slightly confused. "Won't that get a bit smokey and set off all the fire alarms?"

"Nah Glyn, we'll be doing it on the George Foremans. Elaine's brother got a job lot in that he couldn't shift, so we bought half of them off him. We're looking at making it a regular feature. We've got all sorts going onto the grills: ostrich, crocodile, eland..."

"What the bloody hell is an eland?" Glyn asked, now even more bewildered than he was before.

"I dunno Glyn butt, but it looks bloody well lush!" Bob enthused. "Come on down if you want a try. And if we hear anything about than Banksy we'll give you a shout."

"Alright Bob, see you soon matey," Glyn signed off. He let out a massive troubled sigh.

"It reckons here," Kevin cheerfully explained, "that an eland is a kind of massive antelope, found on the plains and savannahs of Eastern and Southern Africa..."

"With all due respect, Kevin, I don't actually give too much of a chuff about what an eland is right now," Glyn said with a mild trembling thunder on his voice. "I'm more concerned about the sudden glut of unwelcome traffic we're going to get up this lane. Because if Bob's on to us, every fucker from here to Fishguard is going to want to come up for a look before we know it!"
"You talked him out of it though, Glyn?"

"Yeah, for now. But seeing as that Banksy twat's published our names for all to see, we're going to get all kinds of freaks and weirdos wandering up the lane once they've put two and two together. And can you smell that?"

"What?" Kevin asked, innocently.

"You're bloody noseblind to it, butty boy! That sweet smell of skunk that's floating down the valley like a groovy cloud. If anyone gets inside a hundred yards of this place they're going to know what's going on. And then things are going to get really complicated for me and you both!"

"Bugger," said Kevin. "Bloody bugger! What are we going to do with all the merchandise?"

"I don't know Kevin lad, but we've got to think of something fast, because before we know it this place is going to look like bloody Oxford Street at Christmas…"

Glyn's phone rang again.

"Hello Glyn? This is PC Alan. Word has it you've got a Banksy…"

7

"Ohhhhh bloody hell, Kevin, it's PC Alan!" Glyn whispered in a panic with the bottom of the phone rammed into his jumper to muffle the sound. "What do I do?"

"Keep calm, Glyn," Kevin whispered back. "Just keep calm. You'll think of something."

"I'll give you bloody calm, Kevin!" Glyn snapped back, "You just…"

"Hello? Glyn?" asked the voice on the phone. "Are you there?"

"Oh hello PC Alan, butt," blustered Glyn, his mind spinning with a number of options of explanation, and most of them too ludicrous to recite. "How's it going mun? And how did you get my number?"

"Ohhh, Kevin's Mam passed it on to me," PC Alan replied. "I thought you might be needing a bit of help?"

Glyn shot daggers with his eyes at Kevin upon the news of this awkward development. But Kevin just mouthed the words "SEE! I TOLD YOU SHE WAS A SPY!" back at him in an exaggerated fashion.

"Help, butt? How do you mean?'" Glyn stalled.

"Well if, as the rumours suggest, it is an actual real Banksy that you've got on your barn you'll be going to need a bit of help controlling all that traffic that's coming up the lane," PC Alan explained. "And where are they all going to park? You remember what happened to that laddie down in Port Talbot when that Bristolian vandal painted up the back of his garage? It was bloody mayhem! If we can put a stop to all that kind of business before it gets going we'll be ahead of the game. And perhaps we can start charging for car parking? It's all part of our caring local police enforcement strategy. You know, nip a problem in the bud before it becomes a big flower, like."

Images of massive crowds shuffling up the lane like artistically dressed zombies flickered before Glyn's mind's eye. He got overly anxious when any of those nerdy hill walkers with their woolly hats and expensive ergo-dynamic sticks came tottering along by the house, let alone flocks of bloody gawping tourists and thrill seekers. And that's before you take into account what's growing in the barn. His chest began to tighten, and his voice cracked a little as he made his reply.

"No PC Alan. It's just some artsy fartsy student type from Bristol who's been up here pissballing about with his spray cans. It's nothing to worry about, mate. We'll have it scrubbed off before you know it," Glyn lied, clenching his non-phone holding hand so tightly into a fist that his nails were digging into his palm and breaking the skin.

"Ahh," said PC Alan, curtly. "You'd better not do that. The bloody thing could be worth millions to some American with a big chequebook and no taste. And I reckon that the local council would want to slap a preservation order on the thing if they get wind of it, so they can try to big it up as some kind of vital local artefact to help bring the tourist money up to this end of the valley. We get precious little of that around these parts as it is. We could be onto a little goldmine here!"

Glyn's eyes began to flicker in panic. All the blood rushed to his head and his breath shortened. Suddenly his whole nice, calm, quiet little world began to crumble around him. His voice wavered as he begun to concoct another bag of hopefully believable lies.

"Nah, it's really nothing, PC Alan,' he blustered. "Just a crappy little bit of tagging. It's nothing to get excited about. And who told you about all this anyway?"

"Ohhh, it was that Bob down the Green Dragon. He reckons his daughter Summer saw something about it on the internet," PC Alan explained.

"Oh you know Bob," Glyn freestyled, pretending to be calm, but absolutely bricking it beneath the surface, like some kind of incontinent swan. "He's prone to these flights of fancy. And he knows so little about modern culture that he's convinced all that porno graffiti in his pub bogs was done by bloody Banksy, too. It's the only name he knows!"

PC Alan let out a rich, hearty guffaw. "Ha, yes, I get your point, Glyn. But I still fancy wandering up the lane at some point over the next couple of days just to check it out and see what's what. You know, to fully assess the situation. After all, I wouldn't be doing my job if I didn't!"

"Of course, PC Alan," Glyn replied with fake bonhomie, "When do you fancy coming up?"

"Ohhhh, how does tomorrow lunchtime sound to you, butty? You got any biscuits in?"

"Of course PC Alan," Glyn answered. "We always have biscuits. Yes, see you then. Bye. Yeah bye. See you. Bye!"

Glyn rang off, flopped the phone gently onto the sofa, stared deeply into the dusty fireplace and sighed for a second or two before getting noticeably agitated. "Shiiiiiiiiiiiiit!" he yelped out. "Shit! Shit! Shit! What the frigging hell are we gunna do Kev? We've got a million pounds worth of shit art on our wall, the most famous artist in the bloody world has plastered our names all over the internets, and PC Alan is coming around here tomorrow to have a look at that useless blob of paint and to talk about poxy parking. PARKING! That's the bloody least of our worries! How the bloody bastard fuck are we going to weasel our way out of this one? It's all gone to shit just because that speccy twat couldn't find a few square inches to spray his poxy world view onto some pit head down the valley. Why me, Kevin? Why bloody me?!"

He looked over to Kevin, who had an uncommonly serene look plastered across his face. Perhaps this was what he meant when he said he became unusually calm in a crisis. Glyn had never seen him look quite like this before, but to be fair, the pair of them had never quite faced a crisis of this magnitude before, either.

"I'll tell you what I'm going to do first, Glyn, before we get into too much of a panic," Kevin stated, in an eerily calm voice. "I'm going to drop that Banksy lad a personal message to see if he might take our names off that Insta post. Then we can work things out from there. I reckon we're so far out of the way from normal civilisation that we've got a couple of days of wiggle room where we can sort ourselves out before anyone actually finds us. That's plenty of time to get our story straight and a plan of action in place."

"Erm, hello?!?" Glyn coughed at Kevin. "PC bloody Alan is coming round tomorrow lunchtime. And he wants biscuits. Is that some kind of code that's telling us that he knows what we've got going on in the old barn? Oh bloody heck this isn't going to end well is it now! And what's more, you can hardly spell your own Mam's name, let alone draught a letter of request to the most popular bally artist on the poxy planet. How's he going to know it's from us?"

"Chill yourself, Glyn," Kevin smoothly replied. "I've got this all in hand.
Dear Banksy…"

8

"So let's have a look at this again," said Glyn, by now in a right tizzy. "What have you put here?"

'Dear Banksy, me and Glyn are everso sorry that we chased you off last night. Had we known who you were we would have invited you in for a cuppa and a chat. Now the problem we have is that you've put our names on your post, and it's giving us two quiet country lane dwellers a bit more attention than we're comfortable with. So would it be alright if you could possibly see yourself to editing that bit out of your Insta note, sir? And I'm so sorry about that whole burning chilli thing in your eyes. Yours most sincerely, Kevin and Glyn.'

"Do you really think he's going to go for that, Kevin? He must get twenty thousand messages a day from fawning little fuckers who only want to know his real name, or get him to do a personal balloon girl for them. He's never going to read it, let alone act on it after what we did to him."

"Just have a little bit of faith, Glyn," said Kevin. "I'm sure we've responded to his better nature here. Click send."

Glyn clicked send, and they both sat there for a moment with a 'what now' kind of expression on their faces.

"So Glyn. I reckon that by the time he reads this and changes it, hardly anyone will have seen it, and it'll all blow over pretty quickly," Kevin said, encouragingly.

"How many people do you reckon have seen it by now then, Kev?" Glyn asked, hopefully.

"Ooh, let's have a look. It says here three thousand two hundred and twenty seven…"
"Shit, that's still too many people. Let's hope that he reads your note bloody quickly now."

"Oh!" exclaimed Kevin, with a more traditional sheen of anxiety dashing across his features.

"What mun?" asked Gyn with deep concern etched like cart tracks across his face. "You're scaring me now."

"Oh! My mistake," Kevin muttered. "That was just the comments…"

"The bloody comments?!!" Glyn yelped. "Three thousand two hundred and twenty seven bloody comments? How many people have actually seen the bastard thing?"

"Ahh. You're not going to like this, Glyn…"

"Then bloody tell me all the same! I've got to find out eventually…"

"Two hundred and fifty three…"

"Oh thank Christ for that…"
"THOUSAND, eight hundred and eighty five views, Glyn."

"You bloody what? That's more than quarter of a million bloody people – in one bloody morning – who have seen the side of our barn and seen our names and are all wanting to come up our lane and have a little shufty at that bastard thing. And there's going to be double that before he takes our names down – that's if he takes them down at all! Our life as we know it is over, mun. Seriously, we're going to have to get the heck out of here somehow before this all gets too sketchy."

He paused for a moment.
"Let's have a look at some of those comments then, butt. Hopefully they'll all say it's unfinished and it looks a bit shit anyway. Bung us your phone here now."

He grabbed Kevin's phone and began to scroll.

'What a perfect piece of rustic folk art you've constructed there, Banksy sir. And the fact that it's unfinished makes it all the more rare. I just can't wait to see it in person!'

'Whoa! Nice one Banksy! Another classic! I'm looking on maps right now to try and see where it is! Can't wait to meet Glynn and Kev. They sound a right laugh!'

'I know that neck of the woods pretty well. Used to go up there a load when we were kids. I reckon if we all put our heads together we could work out where it is pretty quickly!'

'Bag of shite, as usual Banksy you wanker. As soon as we find out where it is, we'll be up with the sponges to deface it in the name of our glorious and late-lamented leader. Lots of the usual love, Team Robbo!'

"Look! Look! I told you!" barked Glyn, now more agitated that Kevin had ever seen him as he bobbed from foot to foot like a schoolboy goalkeeper in need of a really big wee.

"All these rabid Banksy fans are sitting there with their pencils and maps out trying to work out where we are like some kind of massive international super brain. If them numpties on that telly show Hunted can find out where a couple of bland nitwits are in some cab in the London suburbs because they've traced them calling their Mam from a phonebox, someone's as sure as bloody fuck going to track us down up here. I won't lie, Kevin. I've got the serious fear going on right now."

Glyn stopped again, that worried look now carved across his face like lorry ruts on the local common on the last day of the funfair. "Hold up, Kev," Glyn asked, rewinding his brain a little. "What's all this Team Robbo bollocks? And why are they so keen on messing up our barn?"

"Ah now, thereby hangs a tale, Glyn," Kevin answered, rubbing his hands together like he was brewing up a right yarn. "You want the long version or the short version?"

"I reckon the short version is going to be pretty long anyway... so go on then Kev, however it comes," Glyn wearily replied.

"So, back in the early days of British graffiti, King Robbo was one of the first people over here to take on the New York style of painting up tube trains with massive great colourful tags. A proper pioneer he was..."

"A proper vandal, more like," Glyn grunted.
"Well yes, there may have been some people who looked at it like that," Kevin continued, "But take it from me, he was one of the first people who even thought of doing that kind of thing over here..."

42

"Bit of a shame he didn't consider coming up by here and painting all over the sides of my namesake's bloody coaches then, isn't it now. That would have made my childhood a whole lot easier," Glyn scoffed.

"Oh Glyn mun, yes, that would have been tidy darts! Anyway, where was I?"

"Trains, butty. Trains."

"Oh yes. So this King Robbo fella. Nobody knew who he was, but his stuff started cropping up all over London. You could have asked any cabbie who he was, and they'd have told you where halfa-dozen of his best bits and bobs were located…"
"Yeah, and probably said something like: 'The durtee kaaaaaaahnt' in a loud Cockney accent afterwards!" snorted Glyn.

"No, we've been through this before, Glyn," said Kevin in a very school marmy manner, "Not all Londoners are Cockneys."

"Yeah, yeah. Get on with the story will you. This is all getting a bit too Ronnie Corbett for my liking."

"So. Anyways. After a few years of doing this, Robbo either got bored of it, or grew up a bit, or got tired of always hiding from the police. He packed up the graff and went off and started up a family. Most of his stuff got tagged over – as is the nature of the game. But there was one bit down by the canal in Camden that stayed up for years. Just his name, like, in big bouncy letters. But it was considered as canon in the graffiti world, long before all the poncey graphic designers got involved and started to call it street art."

"This is all very interesting," said Glyn. "But what's it got to do with my pa's barn?"

"I'm just getting to that bit, Glyn. Years later, Robbo's massive tag in Camden was starting to look a little worse for wear. A few hardy souls had risked diphtheria to wade across the canal and spray their own poxy little tags on it. And that's when our mate from last night came into the picture."

"Go on," Glyn said, now leaning off the edge of the dusty sofa and getting drawn into Kevin's yarn.

"Yeah, that Banksy had just got to that point of fame when people reckon they are the kings of the world and they can do any bleeding thing that they want. You know, like poxy little bands do when they've had a hit-and-a-half and start chucking tellies out of hotel windows. Any road, I think that Banksy lad was living up that way at that point, and often used to walk past Robbo's old bit of graff. As the story goes, he reckoned he wanted to stake his claim as the new inky prince in town, so he rented out a little boat, paddled over the canal and painted up a pisstake over half of Robbo's tag."

"The cheeky shitbag!" Glyn exclaimed. "I see he's lost none of his winning charm!"
"So, from there on in a massive feud ensued. Robbo was still looked upon as something of a minor deity in the graffiti world by a lot of the old school spray can cavaliers who just hadn't taken to this upstart Banksy and all his cheaty stencil business. Word soon got back to Robbo, who got in his own little boat and painted over the Bristol lad's pisstake, and then things began to get a bit terse."

"I'm not bloody surprised. They seem like a right bunch of cases, this lot!"

"And while King Robbo was doing his paintovers of Banksy's stuff, a bunch of his disciples dubbed themselves Team Robbo, and would go out chucking painty sponges and dripping tins of emulsion all over our boy's most famous works."

"Oh yes, I've seen some of that," Glyn noted. "So them boys are going to come out and try to do our barn are they? I'll get the pitchfork ready again!"

"Ah, but that's not the end," said Kevin.

"I didn't think it would be," said Glyn, wearily.

"In the middle of all this, King Robbo came out of retirement and started to paint up a whole load of new stuff. He was even getting commissions from posh art houses to do exhibitions and shit. Suddenly he had a new lease of artistic life."

"Hang about," Glyn pondered. "How do we know that this wasn't just Banksy himself trying to whip up some kind of fake outrage to try and get himself in the papers again?"
"I seen a documentary on it, Glyn. The fella was bloody massive. Six foot eight and a proper Lahndahner…"

"Not a Cockney then?" Glyn joked.

"Shut it yooo schlaaaaaaaag!" Kevin countered. The pair fell about laughing on their respective sofas.

"So Kevin, I have one question," Glyn asked. "If all this happened and it got on the telly and everything. How come I've never heard of this Robbo lad?"

"Ahhh, well it didn't end well, Glyn."

"I feared it wouldn't. Go on…"

"Yeah, well just as this Robbo was preparing for his first proper gallery show, he was found at the bottom of a stairwell with massive head injuries."

"Oh bloody shit! I feel like I know this fella now, butt. What happened next?"

"It was bad, man. He was in a coma for three years, but never recovered, and died a few years back. He was only 44, mind. Wife and kids too."

"Shit man! Who dunnit though? Did he fall or was he pushed?"

"No one knows, Glyn. No one really knows. But there's always been a rumour going round that he was pushed down the stairs by some of Banksy's more rabid fans. The old bill reckon it's nonsense, mind, and reckon it was just an unfortunate accident. But there's just no telling some people. And there's kind of two Team Robbos, too. There's the legit lot, who are all old graff artists who just want to keep their Robbo's name alive. And there's this renegade mob of his more unhinged fans who just want to obliterate anything that Banksy's ever done in the name of their fallen hero. And I think that's the lot who made that post there now."

"Oh bloody bollocks. So, if it wasn't enough that some famous fuck has painted a shit bit of art on my wall that's going to drag half the planet's hipsters up the lane sticking their noses into our business, and THEN we find out that PC Alan is going to be pedalling up here on his squeaky bike tomorrow lunchtime, but NOW we've got some marauding bunch of crazed loons on our case who want to come up and fuck up our garden. Thanks a lot Banksy, you tosser, you've bollocksed up my life up good and proper. Could it even get any worse right now?"

Kevin's phone suddenly exploded with noise, cracking the already tense moment in two. Both men stared at the vibrating little piece of machinery, before Glyn gestured to Kevin to answer the thing.

""Ello Kevin you smashing little man, how you doing? It's Scarf Ace here…"

Kevin set his face to his most serious anxious scowl and mouthed two words – 'Scarf! Ace!' – to Glyn.

Glyn, by return, silently mouthed just the one word back…

"Fuuuuuuuuuuuuuuuck!"

9

Scarf Face would be the first to admit that he had an absolutely terrible nickname. He first picked it up when he was a young lad selling cheap teenths of soap bar on the mean streets of Croesyceiliog, over between Cwmbran town centre and the bypass. He always used to tie his scarf in a signature style, and so, coupled with his small-scale small-town drugs operation, but full format mouth and ego, the local scallies used to call him Scarf Ace, just to take the piss like. And it kind of stuck. Scarf Ace didn't much care for it, though, but as a small businessman he was well aware of the power of branding, and his given name of Barry didn't quite offer the same kind of menacing cache.

These days though he was a much bigger operation, and pretty much had the run of the drugs trade of not only Cwmbran new town, but the next few valleys across, too. And he was very well aware of Glyn and Kevin's little side hustle, but happily let them go about their business as it made no great dent into his.

He could be heavy when he wanted to be, but most of the time he affected a kind of affable every man tone, which in reality was probably more menacing than if he was down right nasty. Of course, Scarf Ace wasn't exactly the top of the food chain in the local narcotics trade. He reported to some especially unpleasant characters from down in Newport who would gladly kneecap you if you were no more than half an hour late on a payment. And there were stories echoing around The Valleys that they were responsible for much worse.

A couple of years back there was a spate of kids disappearing up around Blackwood. The grapevine has it that there was a liquid acid craze going on, and these kids were offered big gallon containers of the sweet loopy juice at knockdown prices. You know, a bit like wholesale for trade. Then the dealers would come in and take a cut of anything they sold on afterwards. But you know what kids in The Valleys are like, and a few too many of them started to sparkle on their own supply, which cut the profits of the Newport mob substantially. Of course, they'd send the big menacing lads in, but the kids were in no position to pay, and gradually they started to go missing, slowly, one by one. They reckon it was thirteen or fourteen in total, and the story has it that there's a disused pit shaft somewhere around those parts that now resembles a well in a Mexican ganglord's back garden, but nobody's especially keen to go and find out.

Now, all of this happened on Scarf Ace's manor, but you can never get him to say a word about it. There are rumours that he was somehow involved, but no one is entirely sure whether it's the truth, or just a story that he's latched onto to help big up his menace. But obviously nobody particularly wants to press him on the matter. And even if he did make it all up for show, his connections are such that you could easily get yourself into a spot of serious bother by crossing him, despite his cheery, almost cartoonlike demeanour. So when Scarf Ace calls, you really do have to listen.

"Soooo Kevin, I hear you're having a spot of bother with the painters," Scarf Ace proclaimed cryptically. Kevin's mind began to whirr like an old clock spring. He thought that stalling would perhaps be the best option for a moment here.

"How'd you mean, Barry?" he faffed, hoping that it would buy him a little more time to think.

49

Scarf Ace didn't mind Kevin using his real name. The two of them had known each other since school, and although they were never really mates in the true sense of the term, and despite them being three years apart, they always kind of got along, where the other kids used to steer clear of the older, more businesslike child. And Scarf Ace also knew that he could read Kevin like a book, which is why he always called him rather than the more stoic Glyn whenever he had a proposition, or wanted to find something out. Now and again, if Scarf Ace was short on supplies, he'd tap the lads up for a few plants at decent prices. And while his produce came more readily in pill and powder form these days, he occasionally had a little bulk order for jollies of the more bud shaped variety, and would always make the lads his first port of call if anything cropped up.

For their part, Glyn and Kevin really wanted nothing at all to do with the more professional trade, and didn't want to turn up in any chain-of-supply lists in case the more grown up coppers ever came sniffing around these parts, but Scarf Ace was someone that you just couldn't say no to if he came to call, as he was as annoying and tenacious as he was menacing. And to be fair to the lad, he always offered them good money for their stock.

"You know what I'm trying to say, Kev," Scarf Ace replied. "I sees that Bob from the Dragon last night, and he tells me that that painter laddie from Bristol's been over and left you a little present. Nice fella by all accounts. Any road, I understand that if all this gets out to the wider general public you're going to be getting rather a few unwelcome visitors up your way, which may well impinge on your existing business..."

"How'd you mean, Barry?" repeated Kevin, his mind now awash with terrible images of he and Glyn cascading down a lonely mine shaft.

"Well, perhaps you'll want to be converting that old barn into something like a gift shop to mop up the passing trade, like," Scarf Ace suggested. "And you'll be needing to make some room. After all, you wouldn't want the world's finest art critics finding out what you've got growing in there, would you now?"

"Ohhh. Ohhhhhhh. I see what you mean, Barry. A very, very good point!" At that point he panicked, and putting on his best posh voice, proclaimed "May I just pass you over to my business associate…"

Glyn cast him a steely look as his pal began to hand over the phone, and mouthed the words…

"Fuck off will you Kevin, I don't want to talk to that scary c… Oh, hello Scarf Ace. How can I help you? Good weather we've been having, isn't it!"

"Oh Glyn," Scarf Ace sighed. "You know that I want to speak to the monkey and not the organ grinder. How's that old crop of yours looking anyway?"

"Terrible, Scarf Ace. Bloody terrible," Glyn freestyled. "All that snow last Spring brought down the power cables and it left us without electricity one night, and the frost got in and nipped all the buds proper savage like. I tell you, butt, it was such a sorry state that we had to bin it all. We tried smoking a bit ourselves but it was bloody shit – all green and bitter and strange, like. So we took it all out the back and burned it with all the other garden waste. We were just about to start all over again when all this Banksy shit kicked off. So we've buried all the seed out the back and we're jet washing the barn as we speak to try to get rid of the smell before all those poxy tourists start making their way up the lane."

Kevin's face lit up like a puzzled firework. If he was hearing right, his mate had just practically booked them both a ticket for the colliery bottom. He begun to mentally sort out his will, before he remembered that he didn't actually have that much to pass on anyway, shy of a few rare kung fu movies and some battered yet still collectable trainers – and he was planning on leaving all that to Glyn if the worst ever happened, anyway.

Scarf Ace continued. "Oh that's a terrible shame, Glyn. I'm so sorry to hear that. I was going to offer you forty five grand for the job lot and take it off your hands. I thought it only polite to do my public spirited citizen bit and step in and save you a whole lot of bother over the next few weeks. What a shame."

Glyn's face froze like granite. For not only had he just blatantly lied to potentially the most dangerous man within 25 miles, he'd just shot himself in the foot for a nice, if slightly undervalued, pay day. But things soon got worse.

"If that's the case," Scarf Ace added, "Then you won't mind me coming up and having a look at your barn tomorrow. I trust you about your story and everything, have no doubt, but I reckon I might be able to help you out with keeping some of that more, how shall we say, specialist equipment away from prying eyes. I'll be round tomorrow morning about ten, Glyn. That alright with you?"

"Yes sir, Scarf Ace sir. Yeah, we'll be happy to see you and will gladly accept any advice that you happen to give. Nice one, Barry, see you tomorrow then."

"See you Glyn! Ten o'clock prompt!" Scarf Ace rang off, with a blatant grin on his lips.

"Oh bollocks Glyn," Kevin cried, "What the bloody fuck have you just done?"

"Well Kevin," Glyn said with an unnatural calm to his voice. "I appear to have just told Scarf Ace that we've binned this year's crop, and then he told me that had we not done that, he was going to buy the whole lot off us, lock stock."

"Oh shit, Glyn, that's all a bit unfortunate. But he believed you, right?" Kevin asked, hopefully.

"Not a bloody word of it."

"Shit!" said Kevin.

"Yes Kevin, shit. Very shit. Up to our bloody necks in the stuff, we are. And he's coming round tomorrow at ten to have a look at the barn – he says to help us out with our kit, but I just know that he wants to try and catch us out and sink us into the biggest mire of the skankiest silage that you could even begin to imagine. What do we do, Kevin butt. What do we do?"

"I've had an idea, Glyn boy," said Kevin. "First we've got to take the produce up the mountain. It's about mid day now, so we've got 22 hours to start clearing this shit up!"

"How do you do this, Kevin? How do you suddenly snap from, and don't take this the wrong way, an inept ball of insecurities to a man with an absolute plan? It doesn't make any sense, Kev. No sense at all!"

"It's all them years of pondering and fretting about every eventuality, Glyn. Sooner or later one of them's going to happen, and we're bang in luck with this one! Right then Glyn, let's get to work!"

10

Glyn unlocked the big barn doors and let out a big squinty sigh, his eyes taking a moment to adjust to the big bright lights that filled the roof space. This was going to be quite a job. The barn was maybe thirty yards long and fifteen wide, and absolutely stuffed with row after row of pungent green plants, each of them standing a few inches taller than the top of his head. They had plenty more growing left to do, but they were still sticky with the intoxicating stench of bud.

Handily, Glyn had built each row of troughs onto lockable wheels, like big versions of those ones you get on the bottom of office furniture, just in case he ever had to do a quick get away. Sadly this act of uncanny foresight wasn't followed up with any kind of back up plan, and he wasn't really quite sure what he was going to do with the troughs once he'd got them out of the barn. Fortunately Kevin did have a plan. Of sorts.

"Glyn mate, I know exactly where we could put them," he announced confidently.

"Go on, Kev."

"You know that bothie halfway up the ridge towards the dramway…?"
Kevin continued.

"Bothie? Bothie??? What bloody bothie? This isn't bloody Snowdonia, Kevin butt, it's South bloody Wales. No bugger's ever going to want to walk up around here!" Glyn barked in frustration.

"Exactly Glyn. The local council had some of that EU money left over and didn't want their grant to go down the next year, so they bunged up a whole load of bothies about ten years since, in the vain hope they could attract tourists and fell walkers up around these parts," Kevin explained. "Well, we didn't exactly keep much of a welcome in this hillside for these travelling types, so most of the bothies fell into disrepair quite quickly, and half of them got their stone quarried for rock gardens and backyard fish ponds – you know what it's like around here. But this is one of the few that remained untouched. Well, kind of untouched since the sheep got in."

"Ohhhh, I know the one you're on about, Kevin," said Glyn, perking up a little. "The shitty sheep shed up over the way! No bugger ever goes round there, even for nicking. You might be onto something. That must be about a ten minute drive up the hill by quad. I reckon we'll be able to tow most of them up there by sunset. Get the bungees out, we're going on a ride!"

Glyn finally felt a spring in his step for the first time that day as they got the quad bike out of the garage, carefully wrapped all the precious plants in a chain of bungees to stop them tottering off the troughs, and slowly set off up the hill. Of course what was a ten minute ride under normal circumstances was more like a 25 minute slog with their precious cargo in tow. And the sun was just beginning to dip below the horizon when they began their last sluggish convoy up the hill.

"We've got to get this all done quickly, Kevin mate, or they're going to think that we're lamping down the valley if we need to put our headlights on. And that PC Alan bloody hates lampers. If he even suspects that anyone's lamping by here he'll be up sniffing about for certain," Glyn worried.

"And we don't want anyone sniffing around that bothie, if you know what I mean, Glyn," Kevin chuckled, and they both had a nice little laugh between themselves.

For those of you not up to speed with the rural life, lamping is a form of night hunting where the hunters try to track down any nocturnal wildlife that might be skipping about in the dark by using bright torches or bike headlights. When they catch the animals in their beams they're often betrayed by the eyeshine reflecting out of their peepers, and when dazzled often stay stock still in their tracks, until they're either shot or have the longdogs set upon them. And while it's not strictly illegal for rats or rabbits, there's plenty of other kinds of rural wildlife round these parts that get dazzled by the lamps, like hare and deer and foxes, and the local authorities were really trying to stamp it out. The local constabulary were pretty keen on their wildlife preservation, too – well they didn't have all that much else to do shy of chasing scallies out of bus shelters after midnight, to be fair. So any sniff of it in the hills above the village and they'd be up there quick smart to try to put a stop to it. It's understandable then that given the clandestine nature of their produce, the boys didn't really want to be attracting any undue attention up onto that side of the hillside.

They arrived on their last run only moments before dusk properly set in, and quickly wheeled their last trough into the bothie. The shed was absolutely choc-a-block with plants, but the boys reckoned that if they left them there for a couple of days out they'd be out of harm's way, and it would at least give them some breathing space to decide what to do with them after. Glyn screwed a latch onto the bothie's door frame to stop any passing invaders from getting in, and left Kevin to secure it with a padlock. Then they quickly hopped onto the quad and skittered down the hill with what light there was left, hoping that they didn't bump into any hidden tree stumps or potholes on their route, as there was absolutely no way that they were going to put their lights on and attract any attention to themselves from further down the valley.

By the time they arrived back at Daisy Farm it was pitch black, but they'd thankfully made it unscathed. They parked up the quad in the garage, and quickly set about stage two of the great 'Let's trick Scarf Ace into not killing us' caper. The trick, they thought, was to make the old barn look like it had been recently vacated – but not too recently – to hopefully make old Scarf Ace realise that the line they'd been spinning him was the actual solid gold truth, rather than the pack of unfortunate lies that it actually was.

To try and make things a little more believable, Glyn had unloaded the plants and brought about three-quarters of the empty troughs back down the hill to the barn. He spread them out across the floor of the empty building a little further apart than usual in the hope that, without the plants that they were usually heavily laden with, it would look kind of normal all the same. They even took one of the more stunty plants off the trolleys and burned it down the bottom of the vegetable patch, saving some old ashes to cover the newer ones to help give it something of an antique flavour, just in case Scarf Ace had a little wander about. It didn't feel quite right burning down a half-grown plant, but the two lads figured that it was a sacrifice they were willing to take to help avoid any kind of summary violence from their impending visitor. However, they made sure that they stood just close enough to the fire to get the full benefit of its green and bubbling fumes before it decayed into the flames.

The two of them had worked harder than they had done in years to get the crop out of the way, and the barn was now prepped and ready for the arrival of Scarf Ace. It was about two in the morning and they were knackered, settling into their respective sofas in front of The Shopping Channel and quickly subsiding into a deep and comfortable sleep.

11

It was morning, and the boys were indecently wrenched from their slumber by a loud hammering at the door.

"Boys! Boys! You're not trying to avoid me now are you?" came the familiar booming voice through the letterbox.

"Ohhhhhh, Barry," mumbled Kevin, still partially dreaming in one corner of his confused brain. "We had a big one last night, butt. We must have passed out!"

"It must have been, lads," Scarf Ace laughed heartily, but in that kind of laugh where you weren't quite sure whether he was going to hug you or throttle you when you eventually opened the door. "I've been banging on this old door for a good ten minutes now. I could see you daft pair asleep on the sofas through the letterbox, too. Get here now and open the door. And Glyn mate, put that kettle on would you."

Kevin shuffled over to the door, still cracking the sleepy dust out of his eyes, while Glyn stood up, all confused and disorientated, sat right down again, and shook his head for a bit to try and make sense of the world.

"There's lovely!" pronounced Scarf Ace as Kevin finally opened the door. "Now give me a big old bear hug! Cm'ere!"

Scarf Ace picked Kevin up into his broad embrace, and swung him roughly about. Kevin, still mostly asleep, made a half-hearted reciprocal hugging gesture, but looked for every bit like an old family cat who'd been picked up the wrong way round by a visiting toddler and was desperately seeking an escape route. Glyn, his addled brain now beginning to thaw out a bit, shuffled over towards the kitchen stuff and started to fill the kettle.

"Don't think you're getting away without a cwtch!" Scarf Ace bellowed, and grabbed Glyn side on with the kettle still in his hand, and shook him about a bit. The lidless kettle splashed water all over the kitchen floor, so vigorous was Scarf Ace's somewhat unwelcome affection. He plopped Glyn down, who stood there crumpled for a moment, looking every bit like he'd just been folded down the middle. By this point, both Kevin and Glyn began to have grave concerns, because Scarf Ace could be very much like that psycho cat that everyone's Auntie used to have. The ugly brute wouldn't even look at you most of the time, despite your Aunt's protestations about what a friendly little fella he was. But every now and then it would suddenly become inexplicably cuddly, nutting your legs with its forehead and even climbing up onto your lap for a little cosy up. And that's when you knew you were in the most danger, because at any time it could strike, sinking its teeth into your arm, or dabbing its razor sharp claws into your neck, popping out a vein or a tendon or two with the precision of a surgeon. And Scarf Ace was just like that. The times when he was being most friendly often directly presaged some act of extreme violence – either physical or mental. But there were other times when he was just being genuinely nice – you just couldn't read him. But the lads both suspected that something was seriously afoot.

"You got any biscuits, chaps? I could murder a Rich Tea!" Scarf Ace enquired, the two lads a little unsettled by the almost casual use of the word 'murder' in that sentence. Was their old adversary using a cruel kind of neurolinguistic programming on them? Or did he just like using dangerous sounding words willy nilly. Both of the boys' brains were spinning with possibilities, and most of them didn't end especially well.

"That's a bit of luck," said Glyn, with an affected cheer in his voice, "we've just got some of them in. Here, grab the packet."

"Ohhhhh, cheers Glyn butt," Scarf Ace replied happily. "I always said you were one of the good ones."

The atmosphere began to lighten momentarily, before Scarf Ace hauled this happy domestic scene starkly back down to earth.

"Now, about your old barn," he announced, his prior friendliness now brushed aside, replaced by a steely, business-like cold. "Mind if I take a look?"

Both Glyn and Kevin felt their hearts shoot up into their mouths.

"I've always liked a bit of street art – can I have a shufty at your new Banksy?"

Scarf Ace cracked a smile from ear to ear, and the boys both lost a ton of metaphorical weight from their shoulders. They kind of knew that Scarf Ace was shitting with them, like a lion toying with its prey, but it was a temporary release, and the kind that gave them a few extra minutes to fully wake up and formulate some kind of plan. The three men walked through the front garden and out of the gate into the lane, Scarf Ace striding purposefully as he went, while Glyn and Kevin wobbled falteringly, like condemned men on their way to the gallows.

"Ohhhhh, is that it?" Scarf Ace barked, incredulously. "It's not one of his better ones, is it? What's it even supposed to be?"

"Oh it's not finished, Barry," Kevin explained. "We chased him off before he could finish it…"

"Chased him off, you great blithering prats? Chased him off?!!" Scarf Ace bellowed, with a questioning air. "You could have been sitting on a licence to print money 'ere, and you chased him off before he got it done? What kind of quarter-witted fuck dunces are you two?"

"Well to be fair, Scarf Ace, we didn't really know it was him," Glyn added. "We took one look at the old bastard and thought…"

Suddenly Scarf Ace stuck his fingers in his ears and began to sing like a kid who didn't want to hear the football results before Match Of The Day. "LA LA LA-LA-LA LA!"

'But…" started Kevin.

"SHHHHH!" rasped Scarf Ace, his finger now insistently rigid before his lips. "I don't want to bloody know who he is, do I! It doesn't bloody matter who he is!"

Both Glyn and Kevin were rather surprised by Scarf Ace's sensitivity to the arts.

Scarf Ace continued. "It's like The Stig, or the Phantom Flan Flinger off Tiswas, or Basil Brush, isn't it now. My life won't be made any better by knowing who's in the costume, or who had his hand up the puppet's arse! It'll be made worse, in fact. Who wants to find out that your hero is just some random middle-aged bloke that nobody has heard of. It'll spoil the allure!"

"That's a very good point, Barry," Glyn agreed, hopefully trying to get in Scarf Ace's good books.

"We shall say no more."

"What the bloody hell is it anyway?" Scarf Ace asked, squinting at the wall and tilting his head to the left to try and make out what the splodgy mess portrayed.

"Well apparently it's Thatcher, shitting down a coal mine. But were not entirely sure what it all means, to be honest," said Kevin.

"Oh yeah, I can kind of make out her big hook like beak, now that you say it," said Scarf Ace. "But I dunno if I can only pick it out now that you've said it, like them people who reckon they've seen the face of Jesus in a slice of toast or on a dog's arse. Oh no, actually I've got it now. She's got her keks down and everything. Oh bloody hell, this would be brilliant if it was finished, you two prize nerks!"

"Yeah, Barry mate," said Kevin, "but we weren't to know. We just thought he was some student wanker coming up here to have a practise on some out of the way bit of wall who'd lucked on us by chance. And you know very well that we don't want people sniffing around here…"

As soon as the words escaped from Kevin's now trembling lips he knew that he's put his foot in it and reminded Scarf Ace what he was actually up here for in the first place. He tried to bluster his way out of it.

"…normally, like. Erm, it's a bit of luck that we'd already got rid of the plants or things could have got very sticky around here, and that's for certain!"

Kevin always started to speak like someone from a post-war adventure film when he was anxious, and Glyn cut him a quick shifty side eye to try and shut him up. But Scarf Ace had already taken the unfortunate bait.

"Now about all that, boys," he quietened, in a conspiratorial tone. "It's all still smelling a bit herbal essences around here. Are you sure you've gotten rid of those plants, or are you just trying to spin old Scarf Ace a line now? You don't mind if I have a look in your old barn, do you?"

"Erm, not at all, Barry," Kevin squeaked. "I'll follow your lead. Walk on!"

Glyn clocked him another side eye, and the trio walked towards the big barn doors, one man with considerably more confidence in his step than the other two. When they got to the doors, Scarf Ace stood there for a moment, sucking his teeth and fully milking the moment before the big reveal. He flung them open with a dramatic flourish, arms aloft like an orchestra conductor, before sinking a little in his stance.

"Ohhhhh!" he muttered, somewhat disappointedly, "You weren't lying after all, fellas. I fully and wholeheartedly apologise to you both. I was totally expecting to fling these doors open and find the barn still packed tight with green goodness. I underestimated you both, and for that I owe you a massive favour. But why can I still smell the glorious herb so strongly?"

As quick as a flash Kevin piped up. "That'll be the half dozen bin bags of the dry stuff we've got up in the hay loft for our own personal use, Barry. We'd better shift them out of the way if half the world is going to start sneaking up our lane!"

Glyn put his hand to his face and nodded his head slowly to himself. Because not only was that his own personal stash, but it was also his immediate dry stock for the next couple of weeks. He could absolutely throttle Kevin right now for spilling the beans, but he thought he'd better keep things calm.

"Well I'll tell you what," said Scarf Ace, rubbing his hands together in a business-like fashion, "I'll have five of those bags off you for a ton a piece – a monkey for the whole lot of them. Take them right off your hands so that you don't have anything to worry about when the inevitable hordes come marching up the valley. That'll be one less thing to be troubled by, now, won't it."

Glyn knew that this deal was weighted heavily in favour of Scarf Ace, but in this situation it was one that he just had to take him up on. To do anything else would lead to complication layered on top of complication. He still had the rest of the stock hiding away up in that bothie, anyway, and this move would keep Scarf Ace off their backs for at least a little while anyway. He hoped.

"Couldn't you make it six hundred, Barry?" Kevin chirped up, hopefully, as Glyn internally screamed at him to shut the holy living fuck up.

"Don't take the piss, Kevin butt," Scarf Ace replied. Five hundred, take it or leave it."

"We'll take it!" Glyn quickly cried, before Kevin could dig him any deeper into the mire.

"Nice one boys," Scarf Ace grinned. "Now let's count out the money!" he added, in what he thought to himself was a cracking Jim Bowen impersonation, but that the other two lads had clearly failed to notice. He pulled out a massive wheel of notes from his coat pocket, all held in place by a thin yellow elastic band.

"No fifties, please, Barry," Kevin asked, "You know they never take them down the Co-Op!"

"No worries little fella," Scarf Ace beamed. "Have it in twenties. They're all legit, too!" He chuckled to himself as he counted, and the two lads let out an anxious strangled laugh alongside him, like two yes men who'd been called into their boss's office and were trying desperately not to get the sack.

"There you go Glyn, buy yourself something nice with it," Scarf Ace joked as he handed over the cash. "And if youda want any help with security when things start to go a bit chicken oriental up here, just give us a call."

"Will do, Scarf Ace, will do!" Glyn and Kevin gasped out in unison.

"Ohhhh, and a word of advice to you both," Scarf Ace added, seriously. "You've probably gone a bit noseblind sitting in amongst it all the time, but it bloody reeks of skunk up here. You'll probably want to be doing something about that before it gets too busy and people begin to sniff it out.

Anyway, it's been cracking doing business with you to fine fellas today. Let me know how it all turns out!"

"Will do, Scarf Ace, will do!" Glyn and Barry gasped again. The big, bearlike figured stuffed the five fragrant bin bags into the boot of his big old Saab, cut a skilful three-pointer in the passing lay-by, and sped off down the hill, waving from the drivers' window and tooting his horn in a jaunty manner as he went.

The two lads exhaled and slumped their shoulders at the relief of it all.
"Well, that could have gone worse, Kevin. A whole lot worse."

"Aye, Glyn. I reckon we got off remarkably lightly there. I thought he was onto us a couple of times, mind."

"Yeah, that did get a bit hairy now and again, Kev. But I reckon he done us a favour taking them last few bags off our hands. We can stick the one that's left one up in the top shed, out of harm's way, and hope the rats don't get it. Then we can get on with destinking the lane and the farm buildings later, after we've had a bit of a sit down to recover. Get a brew on, Kevin lad. We can have a nice cuppa and a biscuit in front of Bargain Hunt. What time is it, butty?"

"Ten past eleven, Glyn."

"Oh good, we've got plenty of time for a…" Glyn stopped in his tracks and the colour immediately drained out of his face.

"Oh bloody hell," he cried, anxiously.

"What is it, Glyn? What is it?"

"PC bloody Alan is coming around in a minute, isn't he now! Will this nightmare day from scary hell never end?! Quick, get the buckets out – we've got to do some emergency scrubbing!"

12

Glyn and Kevin broke out the mops and hot water and begun to scrub as hard as their pasty little hands would allow them. They got the old barn stinking smashing of Dettol and Jeyes Fluid, and scrubbed the path up from the lane to the house, just in case there was any noxious residue left over from the visit of Scarf Ace. And when they were done they went up the lane a little and started to sniff.

"Ohhhhhh man, Scarf Ace was right. This place still bloody stinks of skunk!" said Glyn, somewhat alarmed. "What are we gunna do now?"

Quick as a flash, Kevin had an idea. "Get the sprays out, Glyn," he suggested. "All of 'em! We'll get this place smelling like that ten yard nasal exclusion zone outside of those Lush shops. You know the ones – them that sell those really stinky soaps and bath bombs and shit."

Glyn nodded.

"I dunno how anyone can work in that place? Man, they can't have any sense of smell left, surely."

"Stop wittering Kevin, and let's get on with it," Glyn asserted.

Kev dashed upstairs to check in all the bathroom cabinets, while Glyn scrabbled around under the kitchen sink. Together they filled up a couple of buckets with aerosols containing enough nasty chemicals to help open up their own personal gap in the ozone layer.

Glyn had a can of Glade in one hand and some Airwick in the other and began to run up and down the lane. Kevin followed him brandishing a canister of Mister Sheen and and a bottle of Febreze, with a tin of Pledge in his pack pocket for good measure.

"We're out here to make this place smell a little less illegal, Kevin," spat Glyn, "Not bloody polish it, you great 'nana!"

"Yeah, but any port in a call, Glyn," he replied. "I just grabbed whatever I could get my hands on."

"I hope you've left my Gaultier Ultra Male well alone, Kev," Glyn cried plaintively. "I only nicked that from the duty free at Cardiff Airport last Easter. I've not got to use it in anger yet, butt."

"Yeah, it's safe, Glyn mate," Kevin assured him. "I couldn't get the plastic off the box in the hurry we're in."

"Thank Christ for that," Glyn sighed.

The pair of them skipped up and down the lane, spraying every last corner of passing air like crazed butterfly collectors jumping with imaginary nets to bring in their quarry. And as the last canister ran out, they stopped to sniff their environment.

"Bloody lovely that is, Kev," said Glyn. "It might not smell natural, but it most certainly doesn't smell of skunk any more. Job well done sir!"

"Nice one Glyn!" Kev replied, before he stopped with a start.

"Can you hear that, Glyn?"

"Whassat, Kevin?"

"That's the bell on PC Alan's pushbike tinkling every time he goes over a pot hole," Kevin suggested. "He keeps it deliberately loose so that any prospective felons can hear him coming and he doesn't have to do any actual police work. I reckon he's about 300 yards away, just around the corner – quick, in the house!"

The hapless pair promptly gathered any discarded spray cans into their buckets and chucked them clumsily into the shed behind the old barn, before diving into the cottage and piling onto their respective sofas, attempting to create an air about them that suggested they'd been there all morning. They could just about make out the loose gravel of the lane popping and crunching under PC Alan's bicycle wheels in the background, and heard his rattly bell tinkle one more time as he parked up by the gate. His big old police boots thumped on the flagstones ten times as he walked up the path from the gate, and there was a slight pause before he knocked on the door.

"Keep it casual, Kev," Glyn warned his pal before he got up to answer it, "And bung the bloody kettle on!"

"On it, Glyn," Kevin replied as he darted up to the big stone sink.

Glyn opened the door slowly, to reveal a beaming PC Alan on the step.

"Smells bloody lovely out there, Glyn lad," PC Alan exclaimed. "What have you two boys been up to?"

"Well, you know how it is, PC Alan," Glyn improvised. "We were bored this morning, so we've been chasing each other up the lane with tins of furniture polish!"

"You pair of bloody mooncalfs!" PC Alan chuckled, well-versed in the kinds of juvenile japes this pair were famous for executing. "Just as long as you've not been sniffing the stuff!"

The three men laughed – two of them slightly more nervously than the other.

"So what can we be doing for you, PC Alan," Glyn enquired, fishing PC Alan's mood for any kind of clue as to what he was really here for.

"Well to be honest with you lads, when I heard that you might have one of them Banksy's on the side of your old barn I was a little worried for you," he explained, with an unexpectedly warm and trustworthy tone in his voice. "I told you what happened down Port Talbot a couple of Christmases ago on the phone, didn't I? Turned into an absolute bloody circus, it did. And I don't want the same thing happening to you daft pair."

"What did actually happen, PC Alan?" asked Glyn, stalling for time while he worked out some kind of plan of attack. "I reckon I only ever heard half of that story."

"Oh it was a right pain in the arse for everyone concerned, butt…"

Kevin quietly chuckled under his breath to himself. His internal voice giggled "PC Alan just said arse! Hee hee!". To him it was like hearing a mate's dad or Nan swearing for the first time.

Although his own Nan could swear for bloody Wales, she could, so he shouldn't be so childishly surprised – especially as he was now nicely into his thirties.

"Don't you remember, though," PC Alan continued. "Britain's most notorious living painter paid a visit to some garages in Taibach, not far from the steel works, see, and left them one of his so called artworks. On one wall he painted a little lad with a sledge catching snowflakes on his tongue. But around the corner he'd painted up a skip fire and all that snow was actually dirty bin ash. I dunno how nobody saw him do it. There's always people rooting round the back of them garages, having a quiet smoke or dumping mattresses."

"Ohhhh yes, it's all coming back to me now," said Glyn, slowly, stalling for a bit more time. "What happened next?"

"Oh it all turned into a right bloody palaver, didn't it now. As soon as people got wind that it was an actual Banksy people started coming from all over to have a look. At first old Ian Lewis who owned the garage didn't mind, but there were people making a racket out there day and night. So at first he put a fence around it to stop people from chipping bits off the thing, then he had to get a security guard in to keep everything calm, and then he had to get perspex shields put up to stop people chucking stuff at it. That actor fella from Baglan – who is he now? Awww yes, Michael Sheen, that's his name – he even helped old Ian out and paid for some of the expense and hassle he had to go through in keeping it safe. But it was still a bit too much for a normal working bloke to cope with. He reckoned that he couldn't sleep with the worry, so in the end he flogged it to the first bloke who offered him some cash for it. And if you ask me he was well shot of the bloody thing."

"How much did he get in the end?" enquired Glyn, suddenly a bit more interested in PC Alan's tale.

"That's just the thing, Glyn butt. Nobody really knows. They said a six-figure sum in the papers, but there's all these art dealers piping up who reckon he could easily have got over a million for it. But to be honest with you I just think he wanted shot of it. But then when he did get shot of it, all these people started moaning at him, saying that it wasn't his, it was Port Talbot's, and he should have left it there for the good of the town. He just couldn't win, the poor bugger."

"So what happened then?" asked Kevin, the two lads now hanging on PC Alan's every word like a couple of kids being told a story by their dad at bedtime.

"Ohhhh, it turned into a right bloody mess, I can tell you. The geezer that bought it off him daubed it all in resin to keep it safe, covered it in a protective frame, and had it lifted out by crane and put on the back of a lorry. Old Ian had to rebuild his shed and all, but you know, the whole thing left him flush. They were the most expensive couple of dozen breeze blocks in all history, them!"

"So, is it all in some American art gallery now," Glyn asked, by now quite wide-eyed with wonder.

"Nah lad, they made a right bollocks of it after that," PC Alan said.

Kevin giggled quietly again to himself. "PC Alan said 'Bollocks'! Ha!"

"That art dealer who bought it off old Ian reckoned that he wanted to leave it in the town for two or three years rather than rushing it off to flog off straight away. And everyone thought that was a decent enough gesture. But the local town council made a right pigs ear of it all. They knocked up this gallery for it, but only opened it for a couple of hours here and there, reckoning that it was too expensive for security and all that. That bloke that bought it wanted to bring all his collection down and turn it into a little museum and put a load of revenue through town, but as far as I know it's still sat in that old shed with nobody looking at it. And who's the bloody winner there, I ask you? Nobody, that's who! My cousin Jeff is on the force down there, and he reckoned that it was a right bloody balls up from start to finish, so I don't want the same thing happening to you lads. That is if it is a Banksy at all. Let's go an have a look at it, shall we?"

The three men got up and filed outside, PC Alan grasping his big mug of tea as he went.

"Oh, you couldn't run back and get us some of them biscuits could you Kevin," the policeman asked. "Rich Tea, weren't they?"

"Yes, no worries PC Alan, give us a mo…" Kevin replied as he skipped back into the farmhouse.

"Now then Glyn boy," PC Alan quietly proclaimed, "You know as well as I do that this is a bloody Banksy. He's admitted as much on his Instawhatsit this morning. When anything like this happens anywhere less usual, the local police forces are alerted to make some kind of an action plan for the mayhem that is likely to ensue. Now, I didn't want to say anything in front of Kevin, as I know he's the worrying kind, but I realise that you might be having some added complications, given all that, how shall we say, produce in the old barn there."

"No no, don't worry, PC Alan," Glyn stuttered, his whole world collapsing around him like a badly built house of cards. "It's only a few old spuds and some apples from the little orchard out back. We store them up to get us through the winter."

"Look, there's no need to kid an old kidder. I know all about your little business. Kevin's Mam told me about it ages ago."

Glyn's brain was now swirling like a maelstrom, utterly unsure of what he could even possibly say next.

"And we don't altogether mind down at the station, to be honest with you."

Glyn now was utterly confused. He was kind of relieved that he didn't appear to be in any kind of immediate trouble, kind of terrified that PC Alan had known about his little operation all along, and utterly terrified about where this conversation could possibly be going next.

"Small operators like yourself are the least of our worries, just as long as it's just the green stuff and you're not moving onto any of those potions and powders. If you're keeping the general local population all relaxed and quelled without turning this all into some kind of major industrial affair, you're good with us."

"Phew, that's a relief," said Glyn, with a release of breath that sounded like one of those big sky balloons burning off some gas. "But what do we do now?"

"Yeah, as long as you don't take the piss, we don't mind if you keep going, just as long as you keep it all on the QT," the officer conspired. "But are only problem now is, what are we going to do with all that stuff in your barn if this place begins to turn into Blackpool Pleasure Beach in the next 24 hours?"

Glyn's mind was a whirr all over again. Should he tell PC Alan what he'd done with his precious crop, or should he try to bluster it out? He figured that the constable had been honest enough with him, and that he should be honest back to him.

"Well actually we're ahead of you there, PC Alan. We took all the stuff up to that old deserted bothie up on the hill over the way and locked it safely in. It should be safe for at least a few days up there now."

"Good, good," said PC Alan. "At least that's a start."

Suddenly Kevin came skipping back around the corner with an unfamiliar packet in his hand.

"I couldn't find any more Rich Tea, PC Alan," he said, enthusiastically. "I reckon Barry must have eaten them all this morning. I could only find some Garibaldi. Will they do you?" Kevin enthused.

"Barry you say?" enquired PC Alan, now sounding a bit more like he was going about his regular day's work. "What Barry's that?"

"Oh, Barry the delivery driver from Mountain Ash," Glyn quickly replied, before Kevin could get another incriminating word in. "He's dropped us off some more Jet Li DVDs this morning. And seeing as it's such a long way out of his way to get them up here, we thought we'd offer him a cuppa for his efforts. It's the gentlemanly thing to do, after all!"

"Ahhh, that Barry," PC Alan replied, his face beginning to warm again. "I thought you meant somebody else. No matter."

"Biscuit, PC Alan?" Kevin enquired, now realising the gravity of his close call.

"If you don't mind I think I'll pass on this occasion, Kevin. I never did much care for the Garibaldi. Too much like a squashed fly sandwich for my liking. But thank you for going to the trouble of fishing them out for me."

"Chuck them here, Kev, I'll have a couple," Glyn asked, now considerably more relaxed. "I loves Garibaldis, I do."

"So," PC Alan proclaimed, kick starting the conversation back to business. "On to the next bit."

"Next bit?" Kevin enquired, suddenly transitioning into anxiety mode.

"It's alright Kev," Glyn replied in a comforting tone, "he knows about our, erm, garden produce…"

"Oh bloody fuck, my Mam's going to kill me!" Kevin panicked.

"Aaaaand I'm completely OK with it – but don't tell anyone I told you that," said PC Alan in an assuring tone.

Kevin's stress quickly flooded out of him, as if he'd been shot like an elephant out of a helicopter by some conservationist on one of those wildlife programmes he loved watching.

"In fact, it was your Mam that told me!" PC Alan chuckled.

Kevin's stress levels began to rise again, sending him into a rollercoaster of paranoid bewilderment.

"See, Glyn, I told you she was a bloody spy!", he flustered.

PC Alan leant in towards Kevin, and quietly uttered some words that he really wasn't expecting to hear.

"It's alright, lad. I was only trying to find out where I could get some old smokey myself. My knees are in a terrible state cycling up and down all these bumpy valleys lanes, and I needed something a little medicinal to calm down their raging a bit. The reason I didn't ask you direct is that I didn't want to shit you boys up and panic you into doing something daft if you heard the old bicycle creaking up the lane."

"Oh that is a bloody relief," said Kevin, coming back into a stationary orbit again, until suddenly a flash of realisation burst across his face.

"Wait! What? Are you telling me that my Mam's your dealer?"

"Well lad, I wouldn't say she's my dealer as such. But she does pass a little of her own supply my way every now and again. It's not just eggs in them old boxes she gives to me, you know." PC Alan gave Kevin a knowing wink.

"Own supply?" Kevin bleated as his brain was fit to explode with utter confusion. "You mean my Mam's a smoker too? Eh? This is all too much to take in on the one day, PC Alan. Take me to the cells. Lock me up for my own safety. I'm done!"

"I'll explain all of this to you in more detail another time, Kevin lad," said PC Alan in a soothing voice. "But right now we've got to work out what do do when this onslaught of visitors come rolling up your lane in the next couple of days. Because if we don't have some kind of orderly plan, we're all going to be in a right bloody pickle. Right, where's this Banksy then?" the officer enquired.

The lads led him out onto the path to show him the half-finished artwork.

"Is that bloody it?" PC Alan said, disbelievingly. "What it is even supposed to be?"

13

Now that the lads knew that PC Alan wasn't the enemy – or at least, most probably wasn't the enemy – they felt they could relax a little more around him, and all settled in around the kitchen table to work out exactly what they were going to do about their little problem out on the old barn wall.

"It may surprise you lads, but all us local forces have got an action plan in place for when anything like this happens," PC Alan explained.

"What, you've got a Banksy plan?" scoffed Glyn.

"Well not entirely a Banksy plan. But a format for what to do if any kind of unexpected artistic incursion suddenly happens in the area," PC Alan continued. "You know, like a Banksy, obviously. But also if some Korean pop star or international social media sensation suddenly decided to broadcast one of their vloggy things from somewhere unexpected."

"Like, when's that ever going to happen around here?" Glyn scoffed again.

"Don't you remember that time last summer when the rumour went around that that Harry Styles from No Direction was sunbathing down Barry Island? It turned out not to be him, of course, but the whole place went into some kind of frenzied hormonal havoc! The poor unsuspecting floppyhaired lad got chased back to his Mam's house by a horde of teeny marauders. And of course, they wouldn't listen to his old man telling them all to piss off, would they now. So the local force had to station someone on their front door for a couple of days until all the hoo-haa died down, and so that all their paintwork didn't get covered in felt tipped love notes and lipstick kisses."

"It's ONE Direction, PC Alan," Kevin politely butted in. "Not NO Direction, ONE Direction."

"Oh it's all the same bloody thing! And anyway what about that Banksy that popped up in Bristol the other Valentines Day. That all got very bitter very quickly, didn't it."

"Oh I don't think I heard about that one, PC Alan." Glyn noted. "What happened there then?"

"Well overnight, up pops this great big picture on the side of a house. A little girl firing off a bunch of flowers with a catapult, I think it was. Anyway, it was bang in the middle of a working class neighbourhood, surrounded by tower blocks and all that. Immediately bits of it started getting nicked, so the building's owners started getting some frames made to cover it up. But while they were doing that, some little local toerag tagged all over it, so they quickly boarded the whole thing up. Then the people who were renting the house off the owners started getting people knocking on their door day and night, asking if they'd seen who painted it, while the owners were getting enquiries from all around the world asking if they wanted to sell it, or telling them their house was going to get vandalised. They had to put up CCTV and a massive big picture frame over it all, and then bat off the local council trying to put a preservation order on it. I tell you boys, it's a poisoned chalice, and a security nightmare at that. It's a good thing you've shifted all your merch already mind."

"Sounds like a bloody nightmare, PC Alan," said Glyn, by now looking more worried than ever. "What can we actually do about it though? As soon as them crazies find out where it is they'll be coming up here by the busload trying to have a look. How can we keep them away?"

"Well for a start," PC Alan suggested, we can actually put a lock on that metal gate at the bottom end of the lanes down by the main road. That'll stop them driving up at least. I'll contact all the other people along the lanes to let them know what I'm doing and give them a key. There's not many of you left up here now, so that shouldn't be too much of a problem."

"Ooh yes, nice idea!" Kevin enthused.

"Then after that, I'll be sure to keep patrolling down the bottom of the lanes, and if anyone asks – because people do always ask a Bobby for directions, it's not a myth – I'll tell them we've never heard of it, and it must be in some other valley. In the meantime, you two boys figure out a way of covering it up without damaging it, and we'll see where we go from there."

"We've got some of that old scaffolding left around the back, PC Alan, from when we did the cottage roof a couple of years back," Glyn quickly suggested. "It's got a load of that green netty sheeting to keep the dust off, too. If we whack that up quickly it might at least stall some of the hopeful passers by, I reckon."

"Bloody good plan, Glyn," PC Allan said approvingly. "Right then, I'm off back down the hill to sort out that gate, now, and I'll keep you posted if any curious looking characters start popping up around the town!"

"We're all a bit curious round these parts, PC Alan," laughed Kevin.

"Ha, alright then, differently curious!" PC Alan guffawed.

"Oh, and when you're down town later," Glyn asked, "Could you pop into the Dragon and tell that foghorn Bob to keep his bloody trap shut about all this? Our lives are in enough of a shitstorm right now without him stirring the pot and making it all more complicated."

"I'll see what I can go, Glyn," PC Alan replied, "But you know the bloody gob on him! He can usually tell me what I'm having for dinner before I get home. I'll give him my serious face when I speak with him. That might work."

And with that, PC Alan drained the dregs of his cuppa and got up to leave. Just as he was throwing a leg over his bicycle and getting ready to trundle down the hill, he stopped and sulked a big shrug.

"Oh bugger, I forgot to tell you," he said.

"What's that PC Alan," the two lads asked as one.

"Me and Mrs Alan are going down to Three Cliffs for the weekend to do a spot of kite surfing, and I'm not going to be here for a couple of days. That PC Graham from Blaenavon is coming over to cover my beat. And you've got to watch him. He's a good copper, and all, but he likes to poke his nose in. I'll tell him to keep an eye out for crazies in town, and that should keep him out of your hair for a bit. Anyway, cheerio lads, take good care of yourselves, won't you now!"

"Cheers PC Alan!" both lads shouted, as they waved him off. "Have a good trip!"

"Well who'd'a thought it, that old pair going kite surfing, eh," Glyn gossiped as soon as PC Alan was out of site.

"They're not actually that old, Glyn," Kevin replied. "I reckon they must only be in their late 40s or early 50s. Proper outward bounders they are. I think it's cute that he calls her Mrs Alan, though."

"How'd you mean, Kev," Glyn enquired.

"You know, it's as if I called my other half Mrs Kevin – if I had one, obviously. I just think it's really sweet."

"Surely Alan's his last name though, isn't?" Glyn pondered.

"Oh, I'd never thought of that. I just thought we called him PC Alan out of fear and respect, and because that's what we called him when we were kids?" Kevin suggested. "And anyway, he said PC Graham was coming over for a couple of days. That's got to be his first name, surely?"

"Graham can be a last name as well, Kevin, can't it?" said Glyn, adding to Kevin's confusion even more. "You know, like George Graham, the old Leeds manager. Or that religious prat, what was it, Billy Graham."

"Ooh, I think you've made a very good point there, Glyn," said Kevin. "I'd never looked at it that way. This isn't going to be another one of them moments like the banoffee incident, is it Glyn?

"Remind me, Kevin. What was that again?"

"Well, for years I thought that tasty sweet pudding pie stuff was named after some obscure village in Italy," Kevin revealed. "I was convinced, mind. Then one day I thought, that must be easy to make, so looked it up on one of those internet cooking channels."

"And then what happened," said Glyn, puzzled.

"So I looked it up and it said something like 'To make this tasty banana and toffee pie, first take three bananas'. And it dawned on me. Banana. Toffee. Banoffee. I can't tell you how stupid I felt when I realised."

Glyn still looked puzzled. "Seriously?" he questioned of his little mate.

"Yeah, I couldn't believe how dumb I'd been!"

"No mate, seriously is it made out of toffee and banana? I never bloody realised!" said Glyn, by now laughing at himself. "I just thought it was some kind of sugary fudge shit?"

"Yeah, toffee, Glyn," laughed Kevin. "At least I know now that I'm not the only stupid head up this lane. I can't believe you didn't know that? I thought you were supposed to be the smart one in this operation!"

"So did I, Kev. So did I!"

The two men stopped and laughed at their own dumbness for a

couple of minutes, before Glyn coughed, pulled his t-shirt straight and announced "Right then Kevin, let's get that scaffolding up! It's all bloody go today!"

"Nice one, Glyn. But before we do that, can I just have a check of my Insta for a moment, to see if that Banksy lad's got back to us?"

"Yeah, good point, Kevin. Good point."

14

Kevin slipped his phone out of his back pocket, and the two lads circled round it, staring through the cracked glass at the tiny screen. As soon as he fired up Instagram, he noticed the little message notice up on the top right of the screen and started to get excited.

"It's him! It's him! It must be him!" he said, all excited, while bouncing about on his toes.

"It's just as likely to be one of them porno models you're always messaging telling you to cease and desist," Glyn laughed.

"Shut up Glyn, I know it's him!" Kevin replied, looking a little hurt. "And anyway, I wouldn't do that…"

"I know, I know, I'm just pulling your plonker," Glyn said, fighting a big knowing grin at the corner of his mouth. "Well go on then, open the bloody thing!"

Kevin clicked on the notice, and it seemed like an absolute age before it opened up.

"Bloody hell, Kevin butt, it's him!" Glyn announced, somewhat surprised. "What does it say man, what does it say? I can't see through all that smashed shit on your screen."

"Hang about, Glyn," Kev answered, "let's get indoors in the shade. I'll be able to have a better look there."

The pair quickly scurried into the farmhouse for a look see.

"Right then, what does he say?" said Kevin, as he scrunched his eyes up and put his face right up next to the screen.

"Lads Lads Lads!' the message started, "Thanks for your note, and I'm so sorry for dropping you two in it. It was a thoughtless move for me to call you by name in my post. I figured you'd enjoy the recognition, but I realise now that my old ego had gotten away with me again. I'm terrible with aftercare – I just usually hit and run and move on to the next one. So I've taken your names down from my Insta post and made the clues a little more obtuse, but I can't take the post down in full, or the Banksy hunters will get even more suspicious. That should give you a couple of days head start to try and sort out your shit. And don't worry about chasing me off. Once my eyes stopped hurting – and what was in that stuff?! – I thought it was pretty funny, and probably less than I've deserved after all these years. By way of apology, I'm dropping you a little something in the mail. You should be getting it in the next few days. Hope it makes up for all the bollocks! Yours, B."

"Well that all sounded friendly enough," said Kevin. "I wonder what he's going to be sending us?"

"Probably a big turd in a box after the way we treated him," Glyn scoffed.

"Yeah, but if he signed it, we could probably get a couple of million for it!" said Kevin, by now laughing his little arse off.

Glyn laughed along with him, and they both pondered the state of the contemporary art scene with a wry smile, before the older lad snapped out of it and set a businesslike look across his face.

"Right Kev, scaffolding. Let's set to work! We've got to get this old bollocks up before sundown, then we can finally have a nice sitdown. All this art world nonsense is proper wearing me out! Who ever knew high culture could be so exhausting."

They both went out to the back shed and started to drag out the scaffold poles and those big clampy things that held them together. Of course, it all began to go a bit Chuckle Brothers, as they'd had professional help putting it up the first time, and they kept narrowly missing walloping each other upside the head with the poles. But despite all their clowning about they were nearly finished, all shy of a couple missing clamps and a couple of scaffold boards that they'd been using for BMX tricks up in the top field, and just as Glyn was doing the final bit of stapling to all that green netting that surrounded the structure, he felt his phone going off in his pocket.

"Who's that, Glyn" Kevin asked.

"Buggered if I know," Glyn replied. "That's not any kind of number that I recognise. Too many numbers, see!"

"Well answer the bloody thing!" Kevin asserted, desperate to know who was on the other end.

"To be honest with you, Kevin, the way our last couple of days have been going, I'm a bit scared to."

"Here, give it to me," Kevin snapped, making a grasping motion.

"No way, mun! Things ain't that bad yet! I'll get it."

Glyn started to drag the urgently vibrating phone out of his pocket and took a deep breath as he prepared to answer. Then it rang off.

"Ohhhhh Glyn you bloody idiot, you let it ring off! That could have been some millionaire art dealer offering us a sackful of money for our old barn!" Kevin sparked off in a highly agitated state.

"Oh, our barn now, is it?," Glyn answered sarcastically. "How many generations have your family lived here for then, exactly, Kevin?"

"Oh you know what I mean, Glyn," said Kevin, a little more calmly now. "Ring it back! Ring it back!"

"Oh I dunno, Kevin butt. That number had so many bloody figures on it that they must have been calling from the moon! Imagine how much the roaming would cost for that!"

The phone vibrated again, and both men instantly stopped their bickering and stared at it hard.

"Answer it then, Glyn, you great big nut!" Kevin barked again.

"Chill your beans, Kevin mun. It's only a voicemail."

"Then put it on speakerphone and let us both have a hear."

The lads sat down on their rickety scaffolding and began to listen.

"Hello! Hi! Is that, errrrrrrrm, Gline there?" the voice bellowed out in an affected, posh, nasal American accent.

"The cheeky shitbag can't even get my name right!" Glyn mumbled in a grump.

"Shhhhh, Glyn butt, I'm listening," Kevin whispered. "And anyway, how's some old Yank going to know how to pronounce our funny Welsh names?"

"Yeah, it's alright for you, Kee-vine!" Glyn mocked.

"Shhh, he's talking again," Kevin snapped.

"So. I hear that you've got the latest Banksy on your wall, and I'd just lurve to see it. I'm going to be in England next week to sell off some old bits and pieces, so I could toddle down to say hello while I was there. Do you think you'd like that Gline? No need to call me back, as I guess you'll be working – or whatever you people do. I can never remember these silly old time differences anyway. I'll call you tonight, shall I? About ten of the clock, your time. Haha! Oh wait, I haven't introduced myself. How terribly rude of me! I'm André Pinchler from New York, and I buy and sell little bits of art and things like that. I'll talk to you later OK lovely. Ciao ciao!" and with that he rang off.

"The cheeky bloody American fucker!" Glyn spat out in a strop. "If it wasn't bad enough that he got my name wrong, then he goes and thinks I'm bloody English too! And what's all that 'Whatever your people do' shit?! The snooty bloody shithead! I've half a mind to call him back and tell him to fuck right off!"

"No no no, Glyn," said Kevin, urgently. "Hold on to them horses. He could easily be our way out of this, with some nice coin in the back pocket and that bloody horrible bit of scrawl on the wall

93

gone for good measure – and before any of them weirdos start ghosting up our lane, at that!"

"I see your point, Kevin. But I'm still not happy about it. Now, let's get this old scaffolding finished and get in for a brew. I'm bloody parched."

15

After about another twenty minutes of clattering and swearing and bruised thumbs, Glyn and Kevin finally slumped in front of their respective sofas and started to muse over all the quite extraordinary events that the last couple of days had brought them.

"Who'da thought it Glyn," said Kevin. "Two nights ago we were quietly sat here watching a nice bit of Jet Li, totally unaware of the highly unlikely chain of events that were about to unfold."

"You're damn right," said Glyn. "I wonder if that Banksy lad ever has any consideration for what's going to happen after he's dusted himself down, packed away his cans and his ladder, and walked away from a job? From what PC Alan was telling us it sounds like it's no kind of fun having a priceless artistic wonder suddenly daubed on the side of your wall. I reckon we've got away lucky that we're located a bit out of the way, and that no one's clocked on to where we are yet."

"Yeah, but for how long, Glyn?" pondered Kevin. "Someone is bound to shop us soon. I reckon PC Alan and Scarf Ace are good for it for a while – well, at least until Barry works out some way to screw money from us, that is. But who else actually knows what we've got up here?"

"That's a point? Who gave that Noo Yoiker art ponce my number?" Glyn wondered. "I'll bet it was that twat Bob again. He just can't keep his bloody mouth shut for five minutes, that lad. He owes me bloody big time!"

"I reckon we're settled for a couple more days, Glyn," Kevin assured his pal, "That is until all the masses get wind of where we are."

"I tell you what, Kevin. Have a look at that picture on Instawhatsit and see if anyone's sussed us out yet."

"Very good point, Glyn! Chuck us my phone over from the side there will you."

Glyn gently lobbed his pal's phone over to him, and he caught it with his left hand.

"Wahey, look at that! I could do cricket, me!" Kevin joyfully exclaimed.

"Stop being a prat, Kevin lad, and tell me what it says."

"Well, he's took off our names from the post, so that's a good start..."

"How many people have seen it now, Kev, though?" asked Glyn anxiously.

"Ooh, about half a million, give or take..." Kevin replied.

"Oh shit!" said Glyn, anxiously. "I wonder how many more of 'em read that note before he took our names off?"

"Dunno, Glyn. But most of his other posts have had millions of views, so it could have been a whole lot worse!"

"Yeah, I guess. How many comments though?"

"It looks like a little over five thousand now, Glyn. But most of them are stuff like 'Another perfect work' and 'Love you Banksy!' down to 'What the fuck is that?', 'Who's that supposed to be?' and 'I just don't get it?' – oh, and this is a good one… 'Did you shag my mum down Lakota in 1989?' Ha! I bet he did and all, the cheeky bugger!"

"Ha! Yeah!" laughed Glyn, before he took up a more questioning tone. "But do any of them say anything about us, Kev?"

"Now let's have a look, Glyn…"

Kevin's thumb went into overtime as he scrolled up and down the list.

"Well, this one bloke here from Belgium here thinks he's onto us…"

"What? No! What does he say?" asked Glyn, the veins bulging in his temples with anxiety.

"I've have worked out where this new Banksy is! Yes I know… " Kevin read loudly in a vaguely European accent.

"Yes? Yes???" said Glyn, even more anxious than before.

"I now know for a fact that it is in Wales!" Kevin continued.

"Twat!" shouted Glyn, half angrily. "Both of you! Did he really say that?"

"He really said that, Glyn," Kevin answered with a coy giggle.

"He must reckon that Wales is a town or something, the great Walloon buffoon?"

"Great what?" said Glyn.

"Oh it doesn't matter, Glyn." Kevin said back.

"OK, OK, so what do some of the others say?" Glyn asked, hurrying Kevin him up from selfcongratulating himself for a joke that he himself didn't fully understand.

"Well they're mostly like those ones we read before, Glyn. Y'know, 'We'll work it out', "I've got a cousin from Wales, he'll know' and 'I reckon it's within ten miles of Pontypool', the usual vague old shit."

"Ha, yeah, the fools!" smiled Glyn, before crashing back down to puzzlement all over again. "Wait. Rewind. What was that last one you said?"

"Oh, hang on a mo..." he scrolled back down with his thumb. "I reckon it's within ten miles of Ponty... shiiiiiiit!"

"How the fuck did they reckon that? Have a look will you?" said Glyn, now with a stark urgency in his voice.

"Hang about, Glyn..." he scrolled some more and read hurriedly for a moment, his eyes scanning every word on the phone in front of him. "Well there's a few people calling him out as a bullshitter, but he's adamant that that bit on your old barn where the roof meets the brick is of a style totally unique to this valley. Nobody seems to be taking him terribly seriously, mind, so I reckon we're alright."

"Yeah, but if one person's worked it out, there's got to be a whole load more clever gits who are a bit more assertive who'll have sussed it as well."

"Ooh yes, Glyn, I reckon you might have a point," Kevin agreed, before slowing down and staring a little more worriedly into his phone.

"What is it, Kevin?" Glyn asked. "You look dead nervous all of a sudden."

"I've just seen another message on here, Glyn, and I suspect you're not going to like it?"

"What is it, mun? What is it?"

Kevin paused for a moment, took a deep breath and stuttered for a moment.

"Erm, yeah, erm, it says 'Glynn and Kev – we're coming to find you, and it won't take us long. Lots of love, the Team Robbo Hit Squad.' Yeah, that doesn't sound too good, Glyn, does it now."

"That bloody Banksy fucker didn't get our names down in time, and that crazed mob are going to be on our case before we know it," Glyn fretted.

"Don't worry unduly though, Glyn," Kevin perked up, with an unsettlingly optimistic tone in his voice. "Old Banksy boy spelled your name wrong for starters, that's one plus point. And for another, there's got to be a thousand Glyns – whichever the hell way you spell it – across these valleys, and probably just as many

Kevins. And that's if they even know where The Valleys are. Half them English knob-ends think anywhere in Wales is called The Valleys, and there'll be even more Glyns and Kevins in all the towns up North. I reckon we're safe for a few days, lad."

"Well, we will be unless they get in league with that brick work bastard on that other message, Kev mun. I thought I was going to finally get a good night's sleep tonight there, but now this has got me in a proper fret."

"I see what you mean, Glyn. I hadn't looked at it like that."

"Can't you get that Banksy bloke to take all that other stuff down though?" Glyn asked. "You and him are mates now, after all?"

"Oh, I don't think we should do that, Glyn mate," Kevin countered. "You've seen how all these people are on here. They'll all think it's some kind of conspiracy if some of their messages start to disappear, and they'll start looking extra hard at what we've tried to cover up."

"Good point, Kev, curse you. What else can you do? Can't you go on there and start making comments to try and start entering some doubt into the equation?"

"Ooh yes Glyn, I could have a look at that. Oh, wait a minute…"

"What is it Kevin," Glyn asked, nervously.

"Well it's my Insta name, Glyn."

"What is it, Kevin. You've not gone and put your whole name and address up there, have you?"

"No Glyn, not quite."

"What is it then, Kevin you nerk?"

"Kev-Wales286."

"Oh you unimaginative twat!" Glyn spat back at his mate. "Why couldn't you have been Sparkle Hat or Princely Unicorn or Wang Monkey or something like all the others?"

"Well, I was feeling rushed, Glyn. I just wanted to get that bit over with in a hurry. And I never imagined that it was ever going to be an issue, did I now!"

"Yeah, I suppose you're right, Kevin. I suppose you're right. Sorry for snapping at you, butt. But yeah, I reckon if you made a comment under that name they'd start to get a bit suspicious."

"Yeah, that's my fear…"

They both stopped in their tracks as a familiar throb rattled about on the stout wooden coffee table.

"Who's that bloody now?" shouted Glyn. "I don't want to talk to any other bastard now after the day we've just had."

He looked at his phone's screen, and that long string of numbers from before was flashing at him impatiently.

"It's that rude American knob again, Kevin," Glyn announced. "You'd better answer it then, Glyn. You'd bloody well better answer it…"

16

"Oh Hi! Gline sir, how are you doing? Good to speak with you!" burst the showy, professionally over-enthusiastic American voice through the phone.

"Yeah mate," Glyn grumbled down the phone. "Is that Dre?"

"André, Gline sir. We don't abbreviate here?"

"Well my name's Glyn, not bloody Gline. I thought that as we were all friends, like, you wouldn't mind if I got your name wrong too."

Glyn made a habit of this. For a simple four-letter name he used to get an enormous number of different misspellings and duff pronunciations – especially in emails. So his tactic was always to spell each errant correspondent's name incorrectly by return, and funnily enough they never got his name wrong ever again. He always imagined them starting to angrily compose a letter explaining exactly what he had done wrong regarding their badly spelled names. But then, just as they'd got going, they'd suddenly realise that they had just done exactly the same thing themselves, and never wanted to speak of it again. Every. Last. Time. It was a small victory, it must be said, but one that gave him great pleasure each and every time it happened.

"Oh I'm so sorry, erm, Glyn, is it?" The voice apologised. "It's that lovely little English accent of yours, it had me all confused there for a minute."

Glyn's eyes flared and his nostrils began to spout metaphorical fire, like a baby dragon who was just beginning to work out how to turn its pilot light on. Of course, anybody that knows anything about the Welsh knows instinctively that the best way to get in their bad books is to call them English. It's like calling a Kiwi an Aussie or calling a Canadian an American – only ten times worse and with a less thinly veiled threat of casual violence.

"I'm not English, you dumbass," Glyn spat down the phone. "I'm Welsh."

"I thought that was the same thing, wasn't it?" questioned the voice.

Glyn was all ready to throw the phone out of the window and go and bury it in a ditch. But Kevin stared at his angry friend, beetling his eyebrows at him in that way that Glyn instinctively knew was code for "Calm down, Glyn mate! Recalibrate! Start again!" Kevin had particularly expressive brows, and you could read a lot of different things from them.

Glyn inhaled a massive breath, let it out slowly, and began to talk, much more calmly than he was expecting to be about twenty seconds before.

"Oh no André, it's a very, very different thing. I won't go too much into the history, but it's fair to say that it's just about the worst insult that you can give to a Welshman to call him English. Now… André…"

Glyn spat the American caller's name out like it was a hot bullet.

"...shall we just go back to beginning of this call and start again?" Glyn suggested with the quiet menace of a man who was at the very last fibres of his tether. "That way we can set off on the right foot again and continue this call in a more civil manner, right?"

Kevin was rather impressed by his friend's assertive performance on the phone so far. Well, after the couple of days that he'd just had it wasn't at all surprising that he was perhaps just a tad on edge. The American caller at the other end of the phone, however, seemed nonplussed and flustered. He sounded like the kind of man who wasn't used to be talked back to. His world was all air kissing and false platitudes, and so he wasn't accustomed to this kind of response. He was almost excited by it a little, but also more than a bit terrified.

So he gathered himself and began to speak. After all, he still reckoned that he could cut himself some kind of a deal out of all this – and he was only dealing with young men from the woods, after all, he figured. "Glyn sir, I'm sooooo sorry for these misunderstandings. My bad. I guess it's a little bit like if you'd have called me Mexican. Oh no, I wouldn't have like that one bit."

"No, that's just actual racism on your part, surely André?" Glyn deadpanned.

"Oh! No! Haha! No, I didn't mean it like that Glyn, haha, oh God no..." the American flustered, a little more anxiously than before.

"Don't worry, butt, I'm only pulling your plonker, you daft twat," Glyn laughed. "Shall we just carry on, now?"

André was now thoroughly confused. There was a bit more regional vernacular in that last sentence than he was prepared for, but at least the Welshman on the end of the phone was laughing and seemed a bit happier than he was before, so he figured he'd just fly with it.

"Ha! Yeaaaaaah, why don't we!" he awkwardly begun.

Glyn quietly snorted to himself, as he realised that he now had the upper hand in this verbal joust.

"So! I hear that you have an all-new Banksy on your property!"

The American's every utterance sounded like it had an exclamation mark on the end of it. So Glyn did what every Valleys lad in his position would rightly do – he turned up the Welsh. And a few notches past eleven, at that.

"Yeah, thass right, butty boy. Ooo told yew that, now."

"Oh my god, what's he saying now?" André's inner dialogue began to ask. "I'll just go along with it and see if I can pick out any words as I go along and work it all out from there. Right. Onwards."

"I'm sorry, what?" the American enquired.

"Who. Told. You. That. Now?" Glyn recited word by word, a little more precisely, and with just a little bit of nark around the edges.

"Ah yes," the American said, relieved "Who told me? Well, when

I saw your lovely little piece of street art on Banksy's Insta I just kneeeew that I had to have it! So I got my people to ring up all the tourist offices in England, erm, and Wales, and gradually, eventually, they found your local office, who then gave us your name! And then we just tried calling every Glyn in the local phone book until we found you. And here we are now! Although, we did get stuck calling up a whole lot of bus companies along the way while we were trying. Do you have anything to do with buses?"

"Bloody hell no, butt," Glyn barked. "Far from it!"

This American seemed to know how to push every one of Glyn's buttons, but it appeared that he was doing it entirely without trying, so he cut him a little slack and indulged him a few more minutes before he told him to piss off. But Glyn's mind did start to wander as he tried to work out just how the local tourist office knew who he was, and how the actual bloody heck he managed to have his personal mobile number in the phone book. But the American soon wrenched him out of all that pondering.

"Aaaaaaanyway," said the American. "This Banksy you have. Do you happen to know what it represents? Because I must say, it's all a little beyond me and my funny New York City ways!"

"Ahh right," replied Glyn. "Well basically it's Thatcher shatting down a pithead – but we're not too sure what it is that's spurting out of her evil arse?"

Again, André's head began to spin as his brain went into instant Babelfish mode trying to internally translate what Glyn had just told him. He gave up trying...

"Who's doing what now?" he queried.

"Thatcher. Taking a dump. Down a mineshaft." Glyn replied, precisely.

"And who is this 'Thatcher' exactly?" André innocently enquired.

"Margaret Thatcher. Our former Prime Minster, and most hated person in the whole of Wales," Glyn answered with utter distain.

"Oooh Maggie!" perked up the American. "I know her, yes. The Iron Lady, so to speak. Meryl Streep. I just luuuurved that movie. I thought everybody over there treated her like some kind of heroine?"

Glyn's fuckwit meter was teetering on the edge of the scale, and his tolerance for this kind of cobblers was fast running out. Kevin beetled his brows at him again, and he resettled a little.

"Oh no," Glyn explained. "Pretty much the opposite of that in every working class area in the country. Apart from those twats who bought their own council house and got shares in BT thinking they were on their way to the land of milk and honey like the posh knobs, the fucking class traitors."

Again, the American didn't quite get the gist of what Glyn was saying, but he could tell that he was angering, so he quickly changed the subject.

"So! I'm going to be over in London town for a few days at the start of next week, and I'd just love to come over and say Hi! And maybe take you out for coffee and have a little chat about your little artefact," the American enthused.

"Out for coffee?" Glyn laughed. "Have you seen where we are on a map yet?"

"Oh no. Just one moment. Where is it again?"

"Just out the back of Cwmtillery, out the other side of the reservoir, butt."

"One moment, Glyn…"

Glyn could hear the American tapping slowly in the background.

"Coom what, Glyn?"

"Till-er-y," he replied, stretching every syllable out for so long that you'd have thought he was hanging his words out to dry.

"Just put South Wales into Google Maps and see what that gets you," Glyn suggested.

"Oh! OK! Yes!!! That works. Yes, you're right, that does all look pretty rustic," the American delighted. "But damn, that's right over the other side of the country from London – what is that, a day's drive? Two days?"

Glyn let out an indignant snort. "No you daft twat. This country isn't as big as your America, like. It's only about 150 miles from London. A three hour drive at a push, mate."

"Oh! OH! I see! I was forgetting that you had such a quaint little country, Glyn! So what's the best way to get there? I'm looking at the map and I think there's something wrong with the text because all of the letters look a jumble."

"No, that's the way everything is spelled around here, André. We've got a whole separate language of our own, you know – they speak it loads up North, although no one much around here speaks it any more."

"You could have fooled me!" André muttered under his breath. "So yes, how do I get there?"

Glyn realised that he could have some futile fun with the American on the other end of the phone.

"Soooooo André. It starts off easy, and then it gets complicated," he said.

"Oh, OK Glyn. So what do I have to do?"

"Right then, turn left out of London, and just drive for a couple of hours until you fall off the end of England,"

"What, really fall off?" the American asked, anxiously, as if he'd been asked to go on some Tolkienlike quest.

"No, no butt, there's a bloody big bridge to go across. But once you're over it you're in Wales, and you have to keep your wits about you."

"Oh yes?" the American questioned, imagining orcs and elves and all that mystical stuff.

"Yeah, because there's a lot of turn offs. So, just as you're coming into Newport, take a right," Glyn continued. "If you go through a tunnel that looks like a shotgun you've gone too far."

This was sounding more and more like a theme park ride to the American with each passing instruction.

"Right, right," he said, "So what's next?"

"Well keep on up that road for about twenty minutes. You'll go past places called Pontrhydyrun and Croesyceiliog and Panteg, but keep going. Loads of bloody roundabouts, mind."

The American's head was now spinning at all these unfamiliar syllable sounds.

"So! When you get to Pontypool, take a left, and carry on down through a little valley, past Pantygasseg and Hafodyrynys, and then you'll come to a T junction..."

"Now hang on a minute!" the American proclaimed. "Panty gas what? You're just making things up and making fun of me now!"

"No, no, André mate. Look at the map. They're all real places. And you're not going to forget them in a hurry. So anyway, at that junction, swing a right, as I believe you lot say. From there, follow the signs to Abertillery. And from there to Cwmtillery. And then you'll see a policeman standing at the bottom of a hill. Just ask him how to get to my house and he'll put you on the right track. We're not on any maps, see."

"Well it all sounds so delightful, Glyn. It looks so green on the maps."

"It is, butt. It is. But I'd better warn you, it is all a bit like the Wild West around here," Glyn warned, conspiratorially.

"How do you mean, Glyn? How do you mean?" replied the now rather worried American.

"I'm trying to think of an equivalent to you, fella," said Glyn, as he strung out the story. "Yeah, you know the Appalachians up in up state New York?"

"Yeaaaassssss?" replied the American.

Glyn was a massive fan of pre-war country music and had been watching all of those documentaries about the birth of American folk song that had been on lately, and knew exactly how to pull his quarry's strings.

"Well imagine that – only in the thirties, and with better drugs!" Glyn exclaimed with undisguised vigour and delight.

"Riiiiight!" said the American, cautiously, knowing full well what the Welshman at the end of the phone was getting at for once. "It sounds, errrrrm, delightful. Yes, delightful! And it's just so very authentic," he added, now chirping up a little. "And it'll add so much provenance to your artwork's value."

"So much what?" asked Glyn, knowing full well what it meant, as he was an avid devourer of Antiques Roadshow and Flog It!

"Oh. Oh never mind. It's an art thing – you wouldn't understand," said the American, dismissively.

"The snooty, patronising bloody arsehole," Glyn thought to himself. "He just thinks that I'm some kind of hick from the woods. I'll show him!"

"So! Yes! I'll be busy at the Tate on Sunday, and I'm at an opening on Tuesday – but I'm free all day Monday if you're available? I'll call you up in the morning before I leave and then we can touch base."

"Right you are, lovely!" said Glyn, jauntily. "We can't wait to meet you then. Ciao ciao!"

The American was suddenly all confused again at this unexpected turn in the conversation style, and he wasn't entirely sure if he was being mocked. He thought he'd better play a straight bat, though, just in case. Because he had to try and prise this priceless artwork out the hands of these rural bumpkins if it killed him. And he had serious worries that it actually might.

"Yes, Glyn! See you then! Looking forward to it," he replied. "Ciao... erm, byeeee!"

And with that, the American hung up. Somewhat relieved that it was all over.

"Ohhhhh Glyn, you bloody bastard," Kevin piped up, rather impressed at the way his old pal had handled the big city art dealer. "You were playing him like an old Stradivarius!"

"Yeah, by the end of it I think he just have thought that he was coming to a cross between Mordor and the Wild Frontier!" laughed Glyn. "And even if we don't get any money out of him, we'll be able to have one hell of a good laugh at his expense."

"Damn straight!" Kevin proclaimed in an overly hammy American gangster voice. "Damn straight!"

17

The next day, Glyn and Kevin woke up in their own beds for the first time in what seemed like an age after a long and well-earned sleep. Well, Kevin was in Glyn's dad's old room, but he stayed over so often these days that it was practically his own bed. The last couple of days had been mind-crushingly complicated and more than a little stressful, but after a day of chatting to an endless parade of decidedly uncalled for parties, the two lads both figured they probably had a day or two's grace before it all got mental again, and treated themselves to a bit of a lie in. Although when you've got a livestock farm to look after, a lie in is more in the region of half eight. Thankfully those sheep could look after themselves, most of the time, so all they had to do was take the quad out with a few barrels of feed and check that none of them had got into any scrapes.

Now, you'd think that there weren't an awful lot of scrapes for a sheep to get into, but his lot were always getting their heads stuck in fences, or trapped in thorny bushes somehow. On top of that, Glyn always had to do a quick patrol every day or two to make sure that any ramblers who'd passed their way hadn't left any gates open or left any litter for his woolly little mates to nibble on and get sick. Fortunately the sheep fields were too far from the lanes for any fly tippers to chuck their tatty building scraps and old broken fridges, but it was those ramblers who were the worst. They were always leaving energy bar wrappers and old plastic bottles laying around – mostly because they'd either got caught by the wind and snapped out of their hands, or had merely dropped out of the back of their poorly zipped up haversacks. But it was always the posh ones that left the longest trails. Fortunately though, ramblers around these parts were few and far between. There were much more showbizy walking areas further north and west, and ones where you didn't have to park up in any working class areas to get to where you wanted to go. The poshies were all too scared that they were going to get their cars broken into to come walking around those parts, the snooty buggers, so would always prefer go to somewhere with a proper car park, rather than leave their family saloons and people carriers outside someone's house and walk up.

But still Glyn would get get the occasional dolt treating his land like their own back garden, so he fuelled up the quad for a quick look see. And of course, he and Kevin also had to pop up the valley to see if the merchandise was doing OK in that bothie, and maybe give it all a quick feed and watering while they were there.

As they made their way up the hillside, Glyn and Kevin began to notice the sheep behaving in a quite uncharacteristic way. Where usually they'd either be just standing about chewing, or skipping happily along after the quad, right now they were either laying on their sides kicking their little legs about, or just staring at the fence poles letting out low, slow, guttural bleats. But then they passed their favourite of Glyn's sheep, a friendly little ram chap that they teasingly called Underbite, because of a massively extending lower mandible that made it difficult for the poor thing to eat in the traditionally sheeply fashion. He'd normally see them coming and race up to the bike to give the trailer a friendly headbutt before running alongside them like a show dog at Crufts. But this time it was as if he'd never seen them in his life before, and was just running around in circles, chasing his tail and letting out a compressed baa that sounded a lot like a stifled giggle.

"Oh bloody hell," said Glyn, concerned. "I've never seen

anything like it! I hope we've not had another crop of them magic mushrooms up by here. It took us ages to get them all down from the trees last time."

"Actually Glyn," Kevin replied, with a worried tone in his voice. "I think it's worse than that."

"Whadaya mean, butt?" Glyn asked, puzzled.

They turned the corner of the top field and the bothie came into view.

"That, Glyn mate," Kevin proclaimed.

It was quite a sight that greeted them. The bothie door was swinging off its hinges, and a polite queue of sheep were lining beside it. Every 20 seconds or so one of their number would skip out quite randomly, often stumbling as it gambolled, and with a familiar far away look in its eye.

"Oh bloody hell, Kev, they've got into the stock! Half the bloody mountain is stoned off its tits!" Glyn yelped, as he hopped off the quad and ran towards the bothie waving his arms about to try to get the fluffy invaders away from his precious herb.

"How'd they get in there though, Glyn?" Kevin enquired anxiously. "I'm pretty sure that we locked it all up, like."

Glyn ran towards the old crumbling brick building in a proper panic, shooing the last few sheep away as he went.

"You know what you've done there, Kevin butt?" Glyn said

disappointedly as he approached the door. "You've shut the padlock around the loop, but you forgot to pull the latch across first. I knew I should have checked it first, but you always moan when I check up on you."

"Yes, I do, Glyn," Kevin replied. "Makes me feel proper useless, it does. But I think you've got a genuine grievance in this instance."

"And now those little fluffy bastards have got in such a drug crazed panic that they've half wrenched the whole bloody door off! I dread to go inside…"

Glyn walked in through the hole where the door used to be and stopped dead in his tracks. Before him was laid out a mild scene of carnage. Trollies were tipped over, pots of his precious cargo had spilled out over the floor, and in the corner sat one sheep, perched up on his tail end like a little man with crossed eyes and chewing a big old bunch of bud.

"Get out of here, you little fluffy white bastard!" Glyn shouted.

"The cross-eyed sheep just looked at him with distain, and an expression that said "Hey man, don't burn my vibe!" or some other hippy nonsense. Glyn grabbed him by the scruff of her woolly neck and hurled her roughly out of the door. The sheep struggled to its feet, turned back to Glyn and gave him the darkest of looks, before it staggered off to wherever it was that sheep go when they're annoyed.

Kevin got to the door and let out a relieved sigh. "Ohhhhh, thank heavens for that. I was afeared that they'd got the whole lot. They must have only just have broken their way in!"

"Or the wind only just blew the, ahem, UNLOCKED, door off its latch!" Glyn sniped. "They've still probably nibbled a good five grand's worth, you daft prat."

He took another quick look at the ragged scene before him, took a deep calming breath, clapped his hands together and said: "Right! Let's get this horrible mess sorted out. I'll start clearing up in here and getting them all fed and watered. You nip back to the house and get my tools. Then we can get this bloody door back on its hinges and get it all fixed up proper and nice and secure so that these nibbly little fuckers don't get in again. They've got a taste for it now, so they'll probably get all MacGyver on us trying to get back in. Took them bloody ages to finally come back down to earth after the mushroom incident. I'll swear these fluffy bastards do more drugs than we do!"

And with that, Kevin motored off back down the hill with a small shopping list of stuff to get out of the barn as Glyn started on clearing up the wreckage in the bothie, booting the occasional ovine invader out of the door as he went.

About twenty five minutes later, Kevin returned with the tools, and they put the door back on its hinges, nailed a couple of battens across its loosening lower slats, and put an extra lock onto it, just to be double safe. After giving what remained of the plants a good feed and watering, Glyn slammed the door shut, made sure that both the locks were securely fastened – triple checking them before he left while looking his pal straight in the eye – and hopped onto the quad to make his way home. As Kevin jumped into the trailer behind him, Glyn turned round with a suggestion.

"It's clear them bloody plants aren't safe up here now – but what can we do with them? We can't have them back at the barn in case them tourists start to poke their nose around…"

"Or Barry Scarf Ace," Kevin added.

"Ohhhh, very much Barry Scarf Ace," Glyn replied. "And it's not long before it'll start getting a bit nippy up here. The leaves will all curl up and get crispy before their time if we leave them up here in the cold. But I dunno what else we can do with them? It's too late to sell them on to Barry, as he'll think that we've been taking the piss. But I don't want to sell them on to any other dealers from down the valley – for one because I don't want to get anyone else involved, and for another, if Scarf Ace gets to find out, and I'm quite sure that he will, then we'll be proper toasted, with a side order of rancid hate marmalade. I really don't know what to do about it, Kevin? I really don't know what to do."

"I'll have a think, Glyn," Kevin said warmly. "I'm reckon there must be something we can sort out. The answer must be hiding in front of us, in plain site, I'm sure of it."

Glyn thought his old pal's optimism was touching, if not a little misplaced. But their minds were both whirring with ideas as they drove off down the hill, zig zagging around the few remaining utterly spangled sheep as they went.

18

As they were packing the quad and all the tools away in the old shed, Glyn and Kevin could hear some muttering and the shuffling of feet coming from the down lane.

"Oh who is it bloody now?" Glyn asked, wearily, and made his way to the front gate.

A couple of kids from Abertillery that he vaguely recognised were walking back and forth up and down the lane, looking puzzled in their knock off sportswear.

"Erm, can I help you gentlemen, there?" Glyn asked politely, with a mock veneer of innocence.

"OH!" the one on the turquoise trackie said with a start, not yet triangulating where the disembodied voice had come from. "Oh, there you are, butt. You half frightened the life out of me! Yeah mate, Bob from the Dragon told us that new Banksy might be up here somewhere, but we can't bloody find it for the life of us!"

Glyn muttered "Bloody Bob!" on his breath, as he craftily sidled along his front garden, raised as it was from the lane, and got between these Banksy hunting kids and their quarry, obscuring their view, and stopping them from getting so much as a accidental glimpse of it.

"Nah, it's not up here, butty," he said nonchalantly. "If he'd been round here we'd've seen him, easy. No one's been up here for days to be honest with you, besides you pair and Postman Pete. Must be up one of those other side alleys."

A gust of wind picked up along the lane, causing a little dust storm. Glyn could hear the netting that wrapped the scaffolding behind him billowing in the wind, and he hoped hard that it stayed true for at least another couple of minutes.

"Oh right," said the one in the dark blue trackie. "We thought it might have been up by here. Sorry to trouble you, mate. We'll be off, then."

"No worries, lads," Glyn cheerily replied. "And if you do find out where it is, let me know would you. I'd bloody love to see a bit of Banksy, me!"

"No worries, pal, we will. See you!" the turquoise trackie said.

"Yeah, bye," said Glyn. "Mind how you go!"

Once the two lads were out of sight, Glyn adjusted the netting and pulled it a little bit tighter, then stormed back to the house with his eyes on fire, like a burning buffalo just set to explode. By now Kevin was back in the kitchen, washing his hands of the day's dirt and filling the kettle.

"Who was that, Glyn butt? And do you want a brew?"

"That bloody Bob!" Glyn bellowed, before calming for a moment. "Awww, yes please Kev. Two sugars, like usual."

His volume instantly ramped up again. "Anyway! That fuckwit down the Dragon has been telling all and sundry that that bloody Banksy shit is somewhere up these alleys. Those two lads might be the first, but they most certainly won't be the bloody last. I've

121

got to get down there and give that old gossip turd a rattling. It's going to be like giro day down the sub-post office up here before we know it if he keeps on like this!"

"I think you'd better calm yourself down first, Glyn lad," said Kevin, trying to extinguish some of his friend's flames of anger, but instead only resulting in fanning them further.

"CALM MYSELF DOWN, MAN?!!" Glyn howled. "I'LL GIVE YOU BLOODY CALM! OK, OK, calm..."

Glyn stopped himself from raging, centred himself for a moment, and took three deep breaths.

"Alright, I've slowed down a bit, but you can see our predicament, here," Glyn said in a slower, more controlled tone. "It's only going to take one of them trackie scallies to tell one bloody tourist what's up here and it'll be like living in a fishbowl over night! Let's get down there and, erm, warn Bob off a little."

"Yeah, but don't you go blowing your top at him," Kevin suggested, gently but knowingly. "I know what you're like when you get het up, and if you go full Ferrigno on him it's not going to help anybody!"

"Good point, Kev," said Glyn, calming even more. "Very good point. But it doesn't help that every time I see his red raddled cheeks I want to slap them really hard. Twice. He gets right up my bloody hoop, that lad."

"Yeah, but softly softly catchy monkey, Glyn," said Kevin.

"What in the absolute bloody bollocks does that mean, Kevin, you twonk?" Glyn retorted, feeling the steam beginning to rise in his pipes again.

"To be honest with you, Glyn, I've got no bloody idea," said Kevin. "But my old Mam says it a lot when I'm going off on one, and it always seems to make sense. I think it kinda means 'calm down and you'll get it done easier' – but she's always coming out with some arcane shit or another. I think she reads too many books."

"Could be, could be, Kevin," Glyn answered, considering what his old pal had just suggested. "But whatever we do we've got to stop that dopey toss rag from spreading the news before it all goes double tits up around here!"

"Good point, Glyn. Shall we walk down?"

"Nah, sod that," said Glyn. "That'll take bloody ages. I'll have calmed right down by then. Let's hop in the waggon."

Glyn went out the front and pulled opened the big double doors of the garage. Inside sat a beautiful old 1969 Commer flat bed truck in a glorious shade of rich pillar box red. Glyn didn't drive it much, as he could easily walk pretty anywhere he wanted to go around the valley, and it was his old man's pride and joy, so he was still to this day a bit nervous about getting a dent in it. But he was in a bit of a rush, and needs must. Both men jumped into the cab and left the garage – although Glyn made sure that Kevin hopped out again for a moment to close the garage doors.

"I can't do it myself, Kevin mun, can I now. I'm driving," Glyn conveniently blagged. "And anyway, we don't want any of them tourists sniffing around in our old garage. Even I'm not entirely sure what's in there."

"Ooh yes, I see what you're saying, Glyn," Kevin chirped, as he dutifully skipped out to get the doors shut.

Once Kevin had hopped back in to the truck again, Glyn looked at his mate and nodded.

"You ready, Kev?" he said, like he was tour managing some kind of space shot.

"I'm ready, Glyn!" his friend replied.

"Then let's goooooooo!" Glyn sung cheerfully, and let the handbrake off.

The pair of them executed this ritual every time they got the old truck out. It was a throwback to the days when they were both young boys, and Glyn's dad used to do exactly this very thing to give the two lads a little cheap bit of excitement. Acting out this simple little task any time they got in the truck helped Glyn think fondly of his old man. He wasn't always in such a terribly dark a place as he was towards the end, and when he was on form he could be one of the funniest and warmest fellows in the whole valley. Or at least Glyn thought he was, and this little thing with the truck always helped him see his old dad through a child's eyes again.

The trick was to see if they could get all the way to the gate by the big road without turning the engine on. He just had to wrestle the gears into neutral, pull the handbrake off and then let momentum do the rest. Of course they always had to hope that they didn't meet any other vehicles coming the other way, or they wouldn't quite make it. And they had to be careful with a couple of the sharp corners and hidden junctions in case they had to put the brakes on and slow it down any, because if they did that they almost certainly wouldn't roll the entire distance to the gate. If the flatbed was loaded up and fully laden they could do it easy. But with nothing weighing heavy on the back it was touch and go as to whether they'd manage to go the whole way.

Off they trundled down the hill, the old waggon slowly picking up speed as they went. It was a little over a mile to the gate, and there were some tough angular corners along the way. They soon passed the two lads in trackies walking back towards town and waved joyfully out of the windows, whooping and hollering like they were extras in the Dukes of Hazzard or some similar American Deep South driving show. As luck would have it they met nobody else passing along their way, and as they rounded the final bend they could see the gate about two hundred yards up ahead of them. The incline of the road started to flatten a little, and it was always a challenge in the final stretch as whether they'd be able to make it or not. But just as the old waggon began to slow on its wheels, the two lads started shushing it on with those jerky hip thrusting movements that we all do in cars when we're going up steep hills to give it the momentum to help it over those last few difficult yards.

"Glyn peered ahead and he noticed something that was a little different to usual.

"Oh bugger, PC Alan must have pulled the gate across. I'll have to slam the brakes on, Kevin."

"No no, Glyn, I think we'll just about make it mate. Just a few more rolls of the wheels." He made that shushing, thrusting moment with his hips again.

"I don't want to be putting a bump on the front of the old man's waggon, mind," worried Glyn. "He'll be bloody furious, wherever the heck he is," he added, first looking to the skies, and then to the ground to cover all the afterlife bases.

"We're going to do it, Glyn, we're going to do it," Kevin shrieked, with the delight of a six-year-old winning his first Scalextric race.

"I've got my foot on the brake pedal, poised like, just in case," said Glyn, cautiously.

The big wheels of the old red truck rolled slowly towards the metal gate, and ground to a halt just two inches shy of it. Kevin and Glyn went berserk in their seats, like they'd just scored a winner in the twelfth minute of added time of some regional non-league cup final.

"I knew we'd bloody do it, Glyn," said Kevin, with a bit too much joy in his voice for a man in his mid thirties doing this sort of thing. "I knew we'd bloody win!"

"Erm not quite, Kevin son," said Glyn, putting on his best serious voice. "The rules of this competition clearly stipulate that the whole of the truck has to be over the finishing line, and we, being two inches behind the line, have clearly failed."

"Oh piss off Glyn, you know we've done it as well as I do!" joked Kevin, as the pair fell about laughing. It had been a glorious release of silliness after the stress of the last three days.

"Well hop out and get it opened then, Kevin," said Glyn.

"Ah yes, I'll be needing to be doing that, won't I, or we won't be going anywhere!"

Kevin skipped out of the truck's cab and walked towards the gate.

"Er, Glyn?" he cried.

"What's up, Kevin butt?"

"It looks like we won't be going anywhere, because the poxy gate's locked with a padlock!"

"You're bloody joking, mun? It's not padlocked like you padlock things is it – you know, like not padlocked at all," Glyn mocked.

"Ha bloody ha!" Kevin replied with a long suffering tone. "Nope, locked solid shut, it is."

"Then how are we going to get ourselves out of this bloody lane then?" Glyn asked.

"Ooh, I'm remembering something, Glyn," said Kevin, with his thinking face on.

"Well spit it out, man!"

"Remember when PC Alan said that he was going to be helpfully locking up the gate to deter any arty invaders from driving up our lane?"

"I remember it well, Kevin. What of it?"

"Well he texes me last night to say that he'd be dropping off the key some time this morning. I do remember that I saw a little brown envelope on the matt this morning, now that I come to think of it. I thought it was a bill or something and that you'd be wanting to deal with it."

"Oh you great blithering prat!" Glyn responded. "First of all, nobody texes anything to anybody, you buffoon. PC Alan TEXTED you. Or he sent you a TEXT. How many times do we have to go over that now?

Kevin had hit a nerve with Glyn. It was one of those irrational sore points that he had that really bugged him, and he could hardly watch EastEnders any more without wanting to throw something at the telly because those mockney bastards were at it all the time.

"Oh, sorry Glyn," said Kevin, sheepishly. "I keep trying to remember."

"I know, I know," said Glyn, before snapping back onto his point. "But secondly, you said that you knew that PC Alan was going to be dropping of a package this morning, and you said that you saw a package on the mat this morning, but you didn't put two and two together and work out that it might perhaps have been the key?"

"Well, it was brown," reasoned Kevin. "I thought it might have been something important. And I know how you don't like me meddling with your mail and all."

"Of course it was something important!" barked Glyn, the veins in his temple looking fit to blow. "It was the key to get us out of this predicament, most probably. And you know that it wouldn't have been the regular mail, because our postie doesn't get around to delivering this high up the valley until well after two."

"Oh yeah, good point, Glyn mun. I didn't think."

"No, that's just it, you didn't think, did you now. Now get back up that lane and grab that key, and you can think about what you've done while you're on your way," said Glyn in a stern and fatherly way.

"Can't we just drive back up there Glyn? That's a bloody long way there and back, after all?" Kevin reasoned.

"I certainly ain't backing up there, butty," said Glyn, only half angrily now. "This lane's too narrow by here to do a three pointer. It'll be like that bit in Austin Powers where he gets stuck in the corridor in that trolley thing if I tried it. And the nearest place to turn is up at that junction about quarter of a mile back. I'd never make it without putting this thing into a ditch or a wall."

"Oh, I suppose you're right, Glyn," said Kevin, with a slug of resignation in his voice. "I'll be back now in a minute."

"And don't you stop to try and scrump fruit off old Farmer Geoff's tree while you're on your way up there," Glyn said, now with half a smile crumpled into the corner of his mouth. "I could see you had your eyes on those apples on the way down."

"I won't, Glyn, I won't," said Kevin, as he trudged back up the lane, passing the two trackie lads about two minutes along.

"Alright fella!" the one in the turquoise trackie said cheerily. "Have you lost something?"

"Only my dignity," Kevin replied, as he shuffled back up the potholed path. "Only my bloody dignity."

19

Glyn could always keep himself occupied while he was waiting for Kevin. After all, it was something that he'd had an awful lot of of practise at. His hapless pal was always forgetting something or another, or losing some vital ingredient of the day's schedule and having to dash off hither and thither to look for it. In all the time that he'd had to hang about waiting for Kevin to get stuff sorted, Glyn had become a bit of a master at the four-in-a-row games on his phone. In fact, he'd spent so long playing them while waiting for his pal that he'd developed something of a sixth sense for what was about to fall out of the sky next. And right now, and this very moment, he was just fixing up a massive link of chain and counter chain that would have propelled him well beyond his already pretty impressive high score. But then he heard one hell of a racket behind him. Pausing the game, grudgingly, just as his numbers were about to go stellar, he dashed his eyes up to the rear view mirror to see what was happening. And when he did he could hardly believe his eyes, so turned to get a better view through the long oblong window in the back of the truck's cab as if he was peering into one of those old What The Butler Saw machines. Only this was way more unhinged than anything those old Victorians could muster.

For there was Kevin, hurtling down the lane on a pushbike like Geraint Thomas on fire. Only it wasn't a normal, grown up pushbike. It was Glyn's old half-rusted Grifter from back when he was a lad. It was already pretty ancient when his old man got his hands on it, so it must have been at least a couple of years older than Kevin himself, and had been sitting out the back of the house getting absorbed by weeds for at least the last twenty years – probably even more. And not only did the chain need oiling, but the brakes had almost certainly packed up a long time since.

"Glyyyyyyyyyyyn muuuuuuuuuun, I caaaan't stooooppp iiiiiit!" Kevin shouted in a blind panic like an on rushing meat-based ambulance as he struggled to keep control of the bike.

"I could have told you that, you daft prat," Glyn shouted out of the cab window as this storm of chaos rolled down the hill behind him.

"As least the incline settles down a bit before the gate," Kevin reasoned with himself, "I'm bound to slow down before I hit the main road, just like the truck did."

Sure enough, Kevin began to slow a little, and he aimed for all the potholes to try to reduce his velocity a little more. But that only resulted in flinging him from side to side across the road on a proper unruly trajectory. He was now only around thirty yards from the gate and still not going anywhere near slowly enough.

Glyn yelled out of the window. "Don't crash into the waggon, mun!", and Kevin managed to steer a course away from the precious red truck, and had practically slowed to a halt when he hit the barrier at the bottom of the lane. But rather than one of those spectacular crashes that you get at the Tour de France where the riders all fly over the top of their handlebars like penguins hopping off an iceberg into the icy waters below, Kevin just tipped up in slow motion, the back wheel now raised almost to the vertical as the front began to crumple beneath him, and landed on his head with a lazy plop on the other side of the gate.

"Bit of luck you landed on the soft bit," Glyn joked out of the truck window. "And anyway, you've bust up my old bike you clumsy git!"

"You've not been on it in bloody years!" grumbled Kevin as he picked himself off the floor and dusted the gravel out of his hair.

"That's not the point," Glyn bickered back. "I might have wanted to sell that on eBay or something. It's an absolute bloody classic that! Whatever possessed you to ride that bloody old wreck down the hill. You could have got yourself killed! Or worse still, dangerously maimed! Imagine having to have your old Mam wiping your arse and your cocksnot for you for the rest of your days!"

Kevin let out a visual shudder.

"I thought we were in a hurry, Glyn," Kevin responded, just starting to get his breath back. "I didn't want to piss you off any further than you already were, so I thought this would save a bit of time."

"Well it certainly did that, butt! Chuck her on the back of the waggon and we'll move off. I assume you remembered the key?"

Kevin frantically patted his trouser pockets in mock trepidation, before looking up with a big grin, saying "Of course I bloody did, Glyn. What do you take me for, eh?"

"It's probably more polite if I choose not to answer that," Glyn laughed. "Go on then lad, get that gate opened, and then get it locked again – properly this time mind – and hop back on the bus. We've got to see that Bob before he spreads any more awkward rumours."

Kevin did as Glyn requested, then threw the old Grifter onto the flatbed, bunjyed it on and skipped back into the cab.

"Ohh, I see you've got that Bubbly Bobbly game going on your phone, butt," Kevin said as he noticed Glyn's device on the dashboard. "Why've you paused it?"

"Well for a start, I had to make sure that you didn't kill yourself, what with you coming down the hill all out of control like."

"You can finish it off now it you want. I'll wait."

"Nah mate, we've pissballed around for too long already," Glyn answered. "And I want to catch Bob before he goes out after the lunchtime rush. And anyway, it's never the same restarting a paused game on your phone, is it now. At the point where you paused it you've built up some kind of incremental stress level where all your high-twitch reflexes are on full alert and you can spot anything, even before it's happened. That's why these games always start so slowly. If you go back into them cold you can never quite get that moment back again and you nearly always crash out in mere seconds. I'll wait until I get back in the house and see if I can get back on it when my head is more settled. I'm still laughing at seeing your silly arse flying down that hill like something out of a considerably more fucked up version of Last Of The Summer Wine! Come on Compo, we've got to get cracking!"

And with that, Glyn rolled the old truck out of the opening of the lane, and after Kevin locked the gate again they headed off towards the Green Dragon. They pulled up outside the old pub, just nipping two wheels onto the pavement. This left enough room for people to get by on the footpath, but also just enough on the other side for vehicles to get by too. Glyn was thoughtful like that, even at times of high distress. The Dragon was one of those pubs where there was always at least three mobility scooters parked outside at whatever time of the day you went by, and the windows were filled with posters for the indoor barbecue later that week.

Bob was always having these slightly off-kilter and hare-brained schemes to try and haul a few extra punters in through the pub doors. Most of them only lasted a couple of weeks before either Bob or the punters got bored with them, though. The best one Glyn could remember was the great meat bowling debacle. Bob had arranged big sides of meat propped up by plate stands on the pin dots of the skittle alley, and charged people a fiver a ball to see if they could knock them over. The concept was simple: if they knocked them over they could keep the meat. It was a bad night for Bob, as all the top skittle players from miles around appeared out of nowhere and absolutely rinsed him for cheap joints. The skittle alley at the Dragon had been out of action for a few years now, though, ever since one of his old skittle team got barred from the league for bringing a broadsword to an away match and threatening the opposing landlord with it when they lost in contentious circumstances. He'd tried putting on the occasional gig on in the alley now and again, but a pub called The Dolls House round the corner pretty much had that line all sewn up, so he jacked that idea in pretty much as soon as he'd started. Since then he'd mostly been using it to store old broken pub furniture that needed a mend and the bits and bobs left over from his get rich quick schemes.

Glyn was just clambering out of the van when he could see the landlord trying to scuttle unnoticed out of the pub's side door. He was a very distinct looking man, Bob. His head looked like he was wearing a mask with his own face on it – only it was three sizes too small and sat on top of a big bag of washing. He had the beetling gait of a fly-half long past his prime, and the biggest bloody feet you could ever imagine on a man of such limited stature.

"Oi! Bob!" Glyn yelped as he clambered out of the truck and onto the pavement. "I've been wanting a word with you!"

Bob clearly heard, but pretended that he hadn't, and nonchalantly kept on walking towards the car park.

"OI! BOB!," Glyn loudened. "I know you can bloody hear me you ropey toerag!"

Still Bob tottered on. So Glyn reached into the cab of the old truck, and from the gully between the steering wheel and the windscreen grabbed what looked like a centuries old bottle of half-finished blue Panda Pop, and flung it in Bob's direction. It was one hell of a chuck, because as it rifled through the air, the stale liquid within making it oscillate in a mad wonky spiral, it flew towards the back of Bob's head as if it was laser guided. Bottle met undersized skull with a hearty 'THUNK!', and passing strangers gave Glyn the unspoken nod of approval, impressed at the accuracy of his aim.

"OW!" yelped Bob. "That hurt, Glyn you daft bastard! Why couldn't you have just given me a yell?"

"You know full well that I did a couple of times, Bob – I could see your ears wiggling!" Glyn laughed. "It was almost like that bit in that video game Metal Gear Solid when the guards get that exclamation mark pop up over their head when they hear some rustling, but instead of dashing to see where the noise was coming from, you were doing a slow runner into the car park."

"I don't actually know what you mean there, Glyn, butt. But I'll take your word for it," Bob replied, rubbing the sore patch on his balding head.

"And anyway, Bob," Glyn added, "why were you running away from me? Anyone would think you had something to feel guilty about."

"I wasn't, I wasn't. I-I-I was just heading up the suppliers, Glyn. Yeah, that's it."

"Now then Bob," Glyn said in his best school teachery voice again. "This isn't an episode of EastEnders, is it. You're not a fictional landlord, unusual as you may look…"

"Hey!" bleated Bob, with a hurt look on his curious face.

"If I may continue," Glyn asserted. "AND you're not trying to trick your missus into not realising that you were going to get sized up for a pair of glasses, or some other unlikely bollocks. It distinctly looked to me like you were doing a runner from me and Kevin, there sir. Now then, can we have a word? In private, like?"

Bob's face sagged into one of those hang dog expressions that showed the lads that he knew he was bang to rights, and slowly walked back to the pub with Glyn and Kevin like a condemned man.

20

Bob led the two lads around the back lane to the old deserted skittle alley, well out of earshot of his wife Elaine, who was running the bar in the pub proper. Elaine was a formidable woman. She had more sense than most of the men in the valley combined, and although she was sunny and friendly most of the time, she had a very low threshold for bollocks, and a bullshit detector that could detect a fib minutes before it walked in the door. All this made her the perfect landlady around these parts, but it also meant that pretty much everybody was just a little bit scared of her – not least Bob, who'd been winding her up with just a few too many batshit schemes to try to pull in the punters of late.

The three men pulled up an old, rickety chair each from the piles leaning against the back wall. Of course, Kevin managed to grab the one with the wonky leg, and went flying backwards as soon as he put his weight onto it. He stood up, grabbed a more sturdy looking piece of furniture, and placed it next to Glyn's to form a kind of inquisitor's triangle, with Bob at the peak of it.

"Don't tell the missus we've been having these words, lads," said Bob, anxiously. "She'll only assume that I've been up to no good again."

"Well in a way, Bob, you have," said Glyn assertively. "And that's why we've come to see you."

Bob's brain got in a proper spin trying to work out quite how he could have offended the two men – after all, he was always winding at least ten people up at any given time, be that deliberately or completely by accident. But it didn't take him long to suss what the problem was this time.

"It's about the Banksy thing, isn't it gents," he confessed.

"Bingo Bobby boy. Bang on the money," said Glyn in his best gangstery voice.

"I'm, I'm sorry lads," Bob apologised. "I just got so excited when I heard about it. And there's so little that happens around here that I thought it might drag a few extra punters in through the pub."

"I can quite understand that, Bob," Glyn replied, surprisingly reasonably. "But that's left us in a bit of a pickle. We're getting all sorts of freaks and strays ringing us up and walking along the lane for a hopeful glance of the dread hieroglyph. And you know how we like to keep ourselves to ourselves, Bob."

Bob knew very well what Glyn meant. He'd been an occasional customer of Glyn's in the past, and loved nothing more than a relaxing jazz cigarette if Elaine was off visiting her sister Linda in Pontypool of an evening. But Elaine absolutely hated that kind of carry on, and didn't want him stinking up the house with those fiery fumes.

"Ah yes, Glyn. I can see your point," Bob answered, now beginning to relax a little. "I guess you wouldn't want too many unexpected visitors up your lane, would you now."

"No we wouldn't," Glyn continued, now fixing him with a steely glare. "But we have. We've already had to ward off PC Alan,

Scarf Ace and a whole flock of tracksuited ne'er-do-wells in the last couple of days because of your big old foghorn of a gob. And lord knows how the local tourist information office got wind of it. Not only that, but they even knew my bloody name! I didn't know we even had a bleeding local tourist information office."

Bob started to look a little sheepish.

"I'm sensing a little bit of guilt steaming up from under your collar there," Glyn noted of Bob as he now squirmed uncomfortably in his chair. "Got something that you ought to be telling us about, mate?"

"S-S-Summer…" Bob stuttered.

"Very interesting, Bob, but it's September now. Summer's long gone." Glyn sneered sarcastically.

"No, no, my daughter's called Summer," Bob explained. "She works over at the tourist information office over in Abergavenny…"

"Oh I should have known it would be over there," Kevin piped up. "Bunch of stuck up yoghurt weavers they've got in that town. Think they're at the gateway to the Brecon Beacons, they do!"

"She was the one who first discovered that picture of your old barn on that Instanet thingy," Bob flustered.

"Instagram, Bob," said Kevin. "Instagram."

"Yeah, that. And to be fair with you we all got a bit excited about it. We thought that the local economy could do with a bit of a cash injection while we had the chance, on top of the extra punters it might draw in."

"Yes Bob," Glyn noted. "But not the Valleys economy. Our own special local economy, like. Did you stop and have a think about how that might have effected us lot up there in the lanes?"

"To be honest with you Glyn, I hadn't," Bob confessed. "I just had the pound note signs ringing round in my eyes. And when that American bloke rang our Summer at work the other day asking after our new artistic arrival I could picture it all playing out before me. We could have sorted out the spare room and turned it into an Air B'n'B for the foreign visitors… started up a special Banksy menu… organised tours and what have you. I never stopped and thought for a moment of the kinds of headache that it would give you. And actually, when you told me that it wasn't on your barn I did actually believe you for a moment – until Elaine told me to stop being such a gullible prat. I feel so bloody guilty now lads, I'm not going to lie. How can I help make it up to you?"

"Well we've got two main problems here, Bob," said Glyn. "One is that we're going to start getting a steady flow of art freaks coming up our lane any day now. And the other is that we've got to hide the, erm, produce before the outside of the house starts to look like the queue at the Louvre to see the Mona Lisa. We've already had Scarf Ace on our case about it. We just want to get it all out of harm's way for a couple of days before we can get it properly disposed of."

"Ooh!" said Bob, with an idea sat pregnantly on his lips. "I might just be able to help you there boys. After we're done with this indoor barbecue larky tomorrow night, our Elaine is off to one of those Licenced Vitular retreats in Swansea until Friday. Every year they have one to teach them all the new accounting techniques and point of sale shite. I went to the first one after we moved here but it was as boring as bollocks. She's always been more of the business woman anyway. So I just sit here looking pretty behind the bar while she learns all the serious stuff that keeps the place going. If you could get all your produce down somehow under cover of darkness on Monday night, we could stash it in here behind all the chairs until she gets home Friday night. We've got plenty of lights in here, too so they shouldn't get too wilty. And if it starts getting too cold I could bung a few of the George Foreman's on to help warm it all up a bit. What do you reckon lads?"

Now although this sounded like a far-fetched scheme, even by Bob's random standards, Glyn figured that it might just work as a temporary move. So the three men sat for a while and figured out the logistics of quite how they were going to get all that produce out of the bothie, through the farm, down the lanes, through the town and into the pub without anybody noticing. But it all looked doable – just about.

Glyn and Kevin got up to leave, and Bob looked considerably more relaxed than he had done at any point over the last forty five minutes. But just as Glyn was walking out of the skittle alley door he turned sharply to Bob, and with a serious look on his face he whispered… "One more thing, Bob. Keep your bloody trap shut until we get all this sorted out, would you now? It'll make all of our lives so much easier, mate."

"Oh you know you can trust me to keep schtum, boys," Bob replied cheerily.

"That's just it, Bob, we don't," Glyn countered. "But in this instance we've bloody got to, or all kinds of kak and complications could fall upon every one of us!" He finished his sentence by miming a zipping moment across his lips and raised his eyebrows enquiringly.

"I'll try my bloody best, Glyn lad," Bob nodded. "I'll give it a real good go."

"You better had, butty," said Glyn and he turned and walked out of the door.

"Do you think he will, Glyn?" asked Kevin hopefully as they walked out to the truck.

"No bloody chance, Kevin!" Glyn replied cynically. "But I think we've put the fear of God up him for a bit. And if he's going to be looking after our produce for a few days it'll behoove him to stop with the old jibber jabber for a bit unless he wants the wrath of the old bill, and worse still, the wrath of Elaine crashing down on him from a great height."

"That's a crafty plan that," said Kevin, impressed at his companion's ever more Machiavellian manner.

The two friends hopped into the truck and began to drive the short journey home. As they crunched their way up the last bit of the lane, they were hoping to have a nice quiet afternoon, just gently sorting out an action plan for the coming days before all the random mayhem fully kicked in. But as they neared the house both men froze in their seats. Because all over the side of the green sheets surrounding the scaffolding were some big bold words written in red spray paint.

"TEAM ROBBO HIT SQUAD!" they stated in capital letters. "WE KNOW YOU'RE HERE AND WE'LL BE BACK SOON!" The word 'Robbo' had a little crown above it in the crew's signature style, and to be fair they'd done quite a decent job of the whole thing, artistically speaking. It was almost a separate work in itself. But the boys had scarcely noticed these more aesthetic concepts as they sat and stared at their new bit of graffiti in increasing horror.

"Oh bloody hell, Kevin," said Glyn."They've found us. What the actual fuck are we going to do now!"

21

Glyn opened the door to Daisy Farm Cottage, and the little brush along its bottom edge pushed two pieces of paperwork across the matt. The first was a colourful card with a few remnants of spray paint spattered across it, while the other was a plain white envelope with a printed label.

"I see Postman Pete's managed to work his way around the gate down the lane," said Kevin, cheerily.

"Yeah Kev," Glyn replied. "But I reckon that top one has been delivered by hand by our artistic invaders out there!"

Both men peered at the floor for a moment, and Glyn stooped to pick both of the items up. The colourful card had a full gloss image of the King Robbo logo on one side, and a scrawly bit of writing on the other.

"What does it say, Glyn?" Kevin asked excitedly.

"I dunno, Kev," Glyn replied, "I've not got my reading specs to hand. You read it out mate."

Kevin squinted at the card, smothered as it was with blobs of red paint and smeary finger prints.

"Sorry you were out. Hope you don't mind, but we'll pop round again on Tuesday if that's OK by you. Hope we didn't leave too much mess, lots of love, TR," Kevin recited.

"TR?" Glyn asked.

"Team Robbo, I'd guess Glyn," Kevin answered.

"Oh bloody hell yes, it's obvious when you see it," said Glyn. "It all sounds a bit polite for a rampaging crew of art assassins, mind. You don't think it's someone from the village taking the piss, do you?"

"To be honest with you, Glyn, I'm not sure that it is. Half the people up this valley don't even know what Banksy's all about, let alone this Team Robbo mob."

"That's a good point, well made, Kev. They didn't sound particularly threatening, though, compared to that big splodge on the scaffolding… Oh bloody hell, they didn't see the actual Banksy though, did they?"

Both men turned on the threshold and rushed back out of the front door and round to the back of the barn.

"Looks like no one's been in there, Glyn," Kevin assured his friend. "The netting's still all nicely stapled, and I can't see any extra splashes or dollops on that abomination on the wall."

"Thank Christ for that," said Glyn, a little more relieved than he would've expected to have been. "If we're lumbered with that poxy thing, we might as well make a bit of cash out of it…"

At that moment, Glyn's phone rang.

"Oh who is it now?" Glyn grumbled. "Oh! It's old Jack Evans from up the lane! He's alright, our Jack. I wonder what he wants?"

"The only way to find out is to answer it, Glyn," Kevin said, deadpan.

"Alright you prat, I'm on it... Hello Jack mate! How's it going? Long time no hear!"

Jack Evans was another of the lane dwellers. If you wanted to find his house, instead of turning right at the top of the hill to get to Glyn's place, you carried straight on for a couple if hundred extra yards and went up an even narrower lane on the left. He originally came from one of those small dormitory towns on the outskirts of London, just on the outer edge of the M25. He used to be a bit of a minor punk rock star in his day, but came down with a nasty little auto-immune illness in his forties, so moved up here to get out of the way of all that pollution spewing out of the city. He was a plasterer by trade, but could turn his hand to pretty much anything in construction. He spent most of his time these days making beehives and fancy letterboxes out of wood. He moved up into the valley as he reckoned that some of his ancestors used to work down the local mines, and he certainly might be half right, as a quick glance around any of the cemeteries around those parts would reveal a sea of his namesakes laid out before you.

He'd often help Glyn out with little odd jobs around the house, and was an absolutely smashing chap. But like pretty much everyone else up the lanes he was also rarely taken to the socials, so Glyn was quite surprised to be hearing from him.

"Yeah, hello Glyn mate," Jack said in his booming estuary English accent. "Have you had any unusual visitors in the last hour or so, fella?"

"How dya mean, Jack?" Glyn answered, cagily.

"Well I've just had a couple of bellends paint some old nonsense all across my garage doors. Something about someone called Tim Robbo or something," Jack explained. "To be honest with you mate I've got no idea what it's all about, but you're up to date with all this modern art shit, so I thought you might. Old Tony up at the top cottage said he had something similar on painted on the side of his haystack when he got back from sorting out the cattle. You got any idea what it might be, Glyn mate? Seems like a bit of a long way to come just to do a bit of vandalism, doesn't it?"

Glyn knew full well what it was all about, but figured that he'd better be a little sparing with the truth for now, just to keep the whole story under wraps for a bit longer.

"Nah, it's probably just kids roaming about and looking for something to do to fill in the gaps between breakfast and dinner time. Every little bugger thinks he's Banksy these days."

"Oh that dopey bastard" Jack laughed. "Good luck to him, I say. But if he comes round here painting on my property I'll be chasing him off with a pitchfork!"

Glyn did a little internal chuckle at the thought of he and Kevin doing exactly to the errant paintsmith. "Ha! I'll bet you would, Jack!"

"Anyway Glyn mate, I just thought I'd let you know. If you hear that anyone else has had their stuff daubed on, give us a shout and I'll let PC Alan know."

"Will do, Jack. See you mate!"

"Yeah, see you, Glyn – goodbye!"

Glyn moved the phone away from his ear and let out a big sigh.

"Right, it's not as bad as we first thought. Sounds like this Team Robbo mob have been speculatively spraying every property along these lanes, probably in the hope that one of us would bite," he explained to Kevin.

"Well that's a bit of a relief I suppose!" said Kevin.

"But the weird thing is," Glyn added, "that they don't seem to be painting their messages of impending doom on anything terribly structural."

"How's that?" Kevin asked.

"Well, they've done our scaffolding, Jack's garage doors – and they needed a new lick of paint anyway – and Gary's haystack," Glyn explained. "I reckon this is just a bunch of kids, gobbing off and trying to look hard rather than any crack squad of meat-headed marauders. I mean, look at that card. If you read it again it sounds just like a school kid wrote it."

"Oh, I see what you mean, Glyn," said Kevin. "But whoever they are, if they catch a dollop of paint all over our new acquisition they could end up costing us a bloody fortune."

"I hate to say it, Kevin, but you're bloody right," Glyn reasoned. "We'd better set to getting that accursed thing properly covered up. Get a couple of rolls of plastic sheeting out of the shed, while I look for some gaffa tape."

"Alright Glyn mun,"Kevin dutifully replied. "Oh, and what was in that other letter anyway?"

"Oh, I'd clean forgotten about that!" Glyn walked back in through the front door, picked the letter off the little side table, and opened it with his big broad thumb. He pulled the letter out of the roughly torn envelope, grabbed his glasses off the kitchen table and began to read.

"Oh bollocks! That's all we bloody need!" he said, glumly.

"What is it, Glyn, what is it?" Kevin questioned anxiously.

"It's from the local council. I'll read it out…"

"Notice of possible preservation order.

It's come to our attention that a new work by the Bristol artist Banksy has been painted on the side of one of the historic barns in the Ebbw Fach Valley. As these barns are unique local cultural artefacts dating back to at least the fourteen hundreds we are consulting with our lawyers to gain legal advice expressly forbidding any of the owners of said barns from demolishing them, in whole or in part, for the purposes of selling on said artwork to investors, private collectors or art dealers.☐With this in mind, we shall be paying a visit to all of the known barns in the valley, in the first instance to list and audit them for historic record and to check upon their general condition, which is something our office has been meaning to do for some years. But secondly to identify which of the barns, if any, is the location of said painting, and to begin to make steps for the preservation of both the building, and the painting, for future generations.

Should we come across any evidence of the recent demolition, in part or in whole, of any such barn, we will take measures to fine the owners a monetary sum as seen fit by the local county courts.

Our visits will be starting on Monday morning, and are expected to continue until late Wednesday afternoon. If you happen to be the owner of said painting, please contact our offices at your soonest convenience and we shall make plans to speed up the auditing process and see you immediately.

We will contact each barn owner by telephone one hour before each visit as the week progresses. We look forward to meeting you all.

Yours sincerely,

Ros Llewellyn

Planning Officer"

"Oh bloody hell,' said Kevin. "That's added another unnecessary complication to the pot."

"Yeah Kev," replied Glyn. "And it was already a bloody horrible soup to begin with! The sly bastards haven't even told us when they'll be coming! There could be all sorts going on up this lane between now and then. What are we gonna do, butt? What are we gonna do?"

"Well, can't we just tell 'em, Glyn? Take it out of our hands and let them worry about it all?"

"Yeah, but it's not their barn that it's plastered across, is it now, Kevin. Imagine having all them crowds shuffling up here, gawping at our wall and bunging empty cans of pop and crisp packets into our hedge. And that's before we even get into thinking about what we're going to do with our little side business. It's frankly all too much to worry about, Kevin. I think my little old brain is going to pop out of my earholes if anything more crops over the next couple of days. That's surely it, isn't it Kevin? There can't be any more layers of nonsense left that we've got to put up with. There can't be? It's like a really shit onion. I don't want to be running a poxy gift shop for the rest of my darned days."

22

Kevin quickly got onto the internet to check out just how many Ebbw Fach Valley style barns there were still left standing.

"They reckon here, Glyn, that there could be anything up to 24 of these barns between Risca and Brynmawr," said Kevin. "They're bloody ancient, too. Centuries old, some of 'em!"

"All these years living here and I never knew that, Kev," said Glyn. "My old man used to say that the shape that all these farm sheds are laid out in probably dated back to Roman times, but none of the buildings are that old, surely?"

"Nah, Glyn, but they reckon here that some of them could be more than six or seven hundred years old!"

"Bloody hell, Kev. And we just batter all our farmyard equipment into it day after day, and grow the unmentionables in it, too! Sounds like it is about time they listed them all – but you can tell how bloody lazy them bastards at the council are that it took until something a bit showbiz happened that they might get a bit of extra cash out of for them to want to actually come round and have a look at them."

"Right then Glyn," said Kevin, restarting the conversation. "Looking at this map here, it reckon it'll take them a couple of days to get up here at least, assuming they start at the bottom and work their way up the valley."

"And even if they start up at Brynmawr, butt," Glyn answered, "I reckon we've got at least a day's grace before they start poking their noses in around here. And of course, they've got to find us first! They won't fancy walking all the way up here now the gate down the bottom has been locked."

"Yeah, good point, Glyn. Bit of a bugger that they're only giving us an hour's notice, mind."

"Yeah, Kev. But that's probably to keep us on our toes, innit. If we chip chunks out of this wall and they start walking up the lane all guns firing we'd be in even deeper shit than we are now. I really don't know how we're going to play this one from here on in."

"I tell you what we've got to do, though Glyn," said Kevin, poised on the edge of a suggestion.

"We've got to stop that tourist information office from spreading, well, information."

"That's a bloody good idea, Kevin," Glyn answered, surprised at his pal's foresight. "Where did Bob say it was again?"

"Abergavenny, didn't he?" said Kevin. "Where do you reckon that is?"

"Oh I reckon that can only be by the market hall or by the museum. I tell you what, Kevin lad. Why don't you pop over there on the bus and have a word with Summer – use your winning charm on her and get her to stall things a bit. Then I'll get old Thatcher bollocks here all covered up safely, and start getting the produce ready for transportation," Glyn suggested, his brain now running into gear like some master strategist.

"Great plan, Glyn!" Kevin chimed, before stopping and looking a little confused. "Oh. I'm brassick mate. You got a couple of quid so that I can get a Dayrider for the bus. That'll save a bit going there and back."

"Oh you tight arsed little shitball, Kev," Glyn replied, before rustling around in his pocket for some change and chucking a handful of loose coins at his pal.

"Here you go, Kev, this should do you! Now," Glyn added, "That Summer is a smart cookie, by all accounts. Don't let her get wind of what we're actually going to do. Make up some cock and bull story about why they shouldn't start telling people about the Banksy yet. I'm sure you'll think of something on the bus journey."

"Yeah Glyn, I'll get my thinking cape on," smiled Kevin.

"Cap, Kevin. Cap!" Glyn replied, his face all screwed up in mild disgust.

"I know, Glyn. I know. gets you every time, that one. Same as the old Damp Squid trick. You just can't resist putting me straight, even though I do it deliberately to wind you up!"

"Most of the time, you little shit. Most of the time," Glyn replied with a scowl.

"Right then Kev, butt. You get on that bus, and I'll get to work by here."

"See you Glyn mate. I'll give you a shout when I'm on my way back."

It was a long old trot to the main road, but Kevin always enjoyed it. The view was different throughout the year, and the colours on the surrounding slopes changed as the day went by, depending on what time it was. And he loved the bus journey even more, especially after it finished zig zagging through all the towns and villages of the valley and got onto the Heads Of The Valleys Road. There was some stunning scenery along that winding route, with proper big mountains to stare at – The Blorenge on the right, The Sugar Loaf on the left, and all sorts of impressive lumps and bumps in between. But today he was a little more distracted than usual and didn't notice the scenery so much, going over and over what he was going to say to Summer in his head. But the more he rehearsed, the more muddled the words got in his brain, to the extent that by the time the bus was pulling into Abergavenny he really didn't know what he was going to say at all. All he knew was that he mustn't say that the Banksy was on the side of Glyn's barn. He mustn't, under any circumstances, say that the Banksy, was on the side, of Glyn's barn.

After a quick wander about the town, Kevin eventually found the tourist information office, although he walked past it three or four times from each direction first, casually trying to peep in and see if Summer was sat behind the counter. Finally, after a brief stop at the bakers to get a nice pasty, he summoned up the courage to open the door and go in.

Summer was sitting behind the desk in her tourist information centre uniform. It wasn't all that impressive. Just a crisp white shirt, one of those splodgy multi-coloured neck scarves that every woman in the service trade seems obliged to wear, a dark blue skirt and a badge with her name written on it in stick-on letters. Just as he closed the door, the sun came out, and shafted beams of light through the shop window, lighting up Summer's hair as if it was woven from thousands of individual strands of gold. Her steel grey eyes, now reflecting the sunlight, were piercing into Kevin's very soul. As he stared at this vision before him, she gently opened her lips and began to speak.

"Ello Kevin love. I sees you walking about outside the shop out there just now, I did. Were you too nervous to come in, bless you? Well you're in now. Well done. I assume that you've come in to talk about that Banksy on the side of your Glyn's barn, have you?"

She delivered the lines like a warm, soft, welcoming machine gun, and together with her beguiling looks and the perfect, heavenly lighting, she looked quite angelic to Kevin's eye. He was never much good at talking to girls, but Summer just put him totally at ease, and before he knew it he found himself beginning to speak, as if detached from the rest of the world.

"Yes!"

The second he pronounced that small but dangerous word he felt like the floor was collapsing beneath him at the burden he'd just placed upon himself. And on Glyn. He knew that Glyn should have been the one to come up here and sort things out. He was better at speaking to women, after all. Not much, mind, but considerably better at it than Kevin was. Fully realising the gravity of the situation, he snapped himself out of his brain swirl and executed the only logical course of action that he could muster, given the difficult circumstances.

"I mean, no!" he said, not entirely convinced by his own words. "Oh, I don't bloody know!"

"Don't worry, Kevin, you silly sausage," Summer sweetly replied. "My dad told me all about it. You know him. Bob from the Green Dragon up in Abertillery."

"Yeah, I know Bob," replied Kevin, his every word now as sticky and difficult to spit out as a marshmallow the size of a tennis ball.

"Well he told me that Glyn had this thing on the side of his wall, but that you wanted to keep it all quiet for a couple of days until you got a couple of bits and pieces sorted out," Summer added at a lightning fast pace. "That's good with us, mind. We can hang on until you're in a situation where you can receive visitors and the like."

Summer gave him a big, knowing comedy wink that could only mean one thing.

"Oh shit, she knows about the skunk," Kevin panicked to himself. "Does every bugger across the whole bloody region know about our stash? It seems like they do!"

"The thing is, see," Summer continued, "when you're all ready and set up, we were thinking of running double bubble bus tours where people come up and see your Banksy first, then head over the hill and spend the rest of the day at Big Pit to go down the old mine and that. How does that sound to you Kev?"

Kevin pondered this proposition for a moment. He reasoned that it actually sounded like a pretty decent day out. Except, of course, for the very good reasons that he and Glyn had for not wanting daily coachloads of slack jawed tourists from who knows where gawping at the side of the barn, and breathing in all those heady aromas from what laid within.

"Oh, I'm not sure that Glyn would like that all that much, Summer," Kevin mumbled. "Can I call you Summer? Is that OK?"

"You can call me anything you like, darling," Summer perkily replied, which gave Kevin warm, uncomfortable, but still pretty pleasurable shivers down his back. "But we could probably do a deal to cut him in on a bit of the cash that we make. Especially if he comes out and tells the story of how it got there."

"Oh I don't think he'll be up for anything like that, Summer," Kevin reasoned. "To be honest with you, he's just after a quiet life, and I don't think he's built for any of that kind of attention. And to be honest with you again, I'm not entirely sure that the painting is worth the trip over. It's a bit rude, and it's not even finished."

"Ooh now, I'll have a little think about that. What's it all about, love?"

"Well we're not 100% sure, but it looks a lot like Margaret Thatcher taking a dump down a coal mine," said Kevin.

"Ewwwwwwwwww!" shrieked Summer. "Now that doesn't sound very nice at all. Why would anybody want to paint that on the side of Glyn's barn?"

"I know!" said Kevin, now relaxing a little. "It doesn't even look much like her to be honest. Just this pointy nose and a strained expression. And if it was finished it would have had a whole lot

of little chuckles dropping out of her and into the mineshaft…"
"I'm sorry," said Summer, stopping Kevin in his tracks, "Did you just call poo chuckles?"

"Yeah, chuckles. Bum pebbles. You know, the kind of things you say when you don't want to say shit in polite company," explained Kevin, now in full blithering flow. "Oh shit, I said shit. Sorry Summer!"

"Oh you're such a little sweetheart, Kevin!" Summer sang brightly, before a sudden gear change powered her straight back into business mode. "Oh, and are you going to my old dad's indoors barbecue tomorrow night? It sounds like a bloody ridonculous idea, but I'll be popping my head round the door so say hello and give him a bit of support. If you're there, me and you can try to talk Glyn into this tourist bus idea. I'm quite sure that he'll go for it if you're on board with the concept too."

"Oh I don't know, Summer. I really think that it's not his flavour of biscuits at all."

Summer chirped like a small colourful bird at Kevin's biscuit analogy.

"He's really not the most sociable of blokes at the best of times, and what with our little business going on…"

Summer gave him that exaggerated wink again. She knew, he was sure of it.

"…I can't see him going for this at all. I can ask him, mind, but I think I know what the answer is going to be."

"Right then, Kevin," Summer said assertively. "You work your special magic charm on him tonight, and we'll see what we can do together tomorrow, eh!"

"Yeah, right Summer, I'll see what I can do!"

"Excellent!" Summer exclaimed, with a happy little double clap. "Right them I've got to carry on here. I've got some leaflets to fold and some commemorative mugs to unpack. I'll see you tomorrow and we can work on him then. Together. Here's my card – I'll write my mobile number on the back. If you have any news for me before the barbecue, just ring and let me know. Right then, see you!"

"See you Summer!" Kevin replied as he walked out of the shop and into the low Autumn sunlight with a small, slightly confused smile upon his lips.

It wasn't until he was almost halfway home on the bus that he'd realised that he'd agreed to help Summer in a way that he wasn't entirely comfortable with. He'd just been sat there, bobbing up and down and swaying about with the vehicle's every movement, trying to work out whether what Summer had just set out counted as an actual date or not when he realised that he might have been rather cleverly played.

"Hold on a minute!" he said to himself as his brain defluffed and clicked starkly into thinking mode, "I never said that I agreed to helping Summer get Glyn on board, did I? Oh shit, I think I might have!" his brain continued. "I don't even want those bloody bus trips to go ahead myself, and Glyn's going to absolutely hate the pants off of the idea. But there's Summer now, thinking that I'm going to tell him that I'm on board with this dumb-ass tour, and that I'm going to try and convince him that he should go for it! That's not going to happen in any shape or form! How the heck did I just let myself get talked into that?! I'm rubbish with women, me!"

And with that, the bus turned into Abertillery and was nearly at Kevin's stop. He'd need that walk back up the hill to work out his plan about how to tell Glyn that he'd been hoodwinked into giving away all the goods, and how to tell Summer that he wasn't even interested in helping her out with her little scheme. He was reasonably sure at this point that she wasn't actually interested in him in the traditional sense of the word, but there was still a little hopeful light flickering at the back of his brain, telling him "Maybe she does like you, Kev! Maybe this is just a plan for her to get nearer to you!" Kevin had long learned to ignore these flickerings as the source of much awkwardness and pain, but he couldn't help but get a little flustered at the thought of seeing Summer again tomorrow. Just in case, like.

23

As Kevin walked back up the lane, he could see a few more people than were usual milling about and looking lost. And what was usual for these parts tended to be only around three or four people a week who didn't actually live up there. Most of the time any passers by were just hikers tooled up for a good ramble, but Kevin must have passed a good half-dozen hipster types with colourful shirts and ironic satchels on his way back up to Daisy Farm. One especially puzzled looking couple stopped him for directions. They were clearly Welsh, but also clearly not from round these parts.

"Excuse me fella," a chap with round spectacles and a plaited beard asked, "do you know where that Banksy we keep hearing about is supposed to be?"

"Cardiff, I reckon!" Kevin surmised to himself, as he worked out where he reckoned these latest lane invaders came from.

"Only we've come up from Cardiff…"

"Yessssss!" said Kevin, internally, as he gave himself an imaginary fist bump.

"…for a look at it after we worked out some of the clues on Instagram. We feel that we can't be far from it now?" the hipster explained.

"I dunno butt," Kevin said, lying through his teeth. "Nothing up here, now. It's so quiet up here we'd have definitely seen something. Although, I've heard it's down by Crosskeys, about ten miles south of here."

"Ooh, that sounds feasible! We'll have to look into that. Right, thanks for the tips!"

And with that, the couple turned on their heels and started to head back down the hill. In the background, Kevin could hear the strangely bearded one chatting to his partner in crime, a woman in brown dungarees with cartoon dinosaurs printed all over them, a silver t-shirt and a big red bobble hat.

"Florence, I told you it wasn't up here! Get the map up on your phone and let's work out how to get to Crosskeys."

Kevin chuckled to himself at a job well done, but couldn't resist giving the knife one last twist, as he turned back to the couple and shouted: "Ohhhhh, and if you find out where it is, do let me know. I'd love to have a look at that!"

"Right you are sir!" the bearded one replied. "Cheers!"

"Bloody Florence!" Kevin chuckled to himself. "It's changed in Cardiff since I used to go down there, I can tell you!"

As he approached the barn Kevin could see Glyn in front of the scaffolding, splashing Team Robbo's old scrawl off with his jetwash. He went over the story of what had just happened with Summer in Abergavenny in his mind before he tried to explain it to Glyn until he'd probably over rehearsed it a bit too much again.

"Oh aye, Kevin lad," Glyn shouted cheerily as he saw his pal coming up the street. "How did you get on with Summer?"

All the blood rushed to Kevin's eyes, and the lane suddenly swooshed with dots of colour, like someone had injected Disney's Fantasia into his optic nerve. What was he going to tell Glyn about his abject failure at keeping this whole sorry farrago quiet? He quickly tried to cook up a scheme.

"She knows, butt!" Kevin nervously spluttered out.

"Shit!" said Kevin's internal self. "Again!"

"You what, Kevin," Glyn asked, looking a little concerned.

"She already knew that we had the Banksy on our barn," Kevin tried to explain. "Or at least she said she did!"

"Bugger!" Glyn spat. "Has she said what she's going to do about it yet?"

"Ahh!" Kevin stalled. "That's the next bit of the problem..."

"I'm not liking the sound of this, Kevin," said Glyn, now looking even more worried than before.

"Please tell me that this isn't going to be shit."

"Well, it kind of is, Glyn, and it kind of isn't."

"Go on..."

"Well, what Summer said was was that the tourist office want to detour the bus trips to Big Pit up by here, to give the punters a little bit of local colour and culture first..."

166

"Fuuuuuuuuck!" Glyn gasped.

"...and what's more, she wants you to give a little talk about how it all came to be," Kevin continued.

"Wha?" said Glyn, now exasperated. "No bloody way, mun. Not in a millions years! I'm not some kind of performing pony!"

"That's what I told her you'd say. But she seems to think that I'm going to try and trick you round and help change your mind. I can't be sure, but I think she was already designing the leaflets, Glyn."

"And what made her think that you were going to help her out there, Kevin boy?" questioned Glyn.

"You didn't swoon at the face of a fine woman again did you?"

"Hmmm..." Kevin mumbled, awkwardly.

"What's that, Kevin?" Glyn asked, a little bit louder now.

"I might have done... a little bit..."

"Oh you little tit!" Glyn laughed at his now squirming friend. "Never mind butt, she'll never talk me round to this."

"That's what I said, Glyn. But she's going to try to convince you about it all tomorrow at Bob's indoor barbecue, isn't it," Kevin spurted out.

"Hold on there a moment! Rewind the record, DJ! What did you just say?" Glyn asked, suddenly looking a bit serious again.

"Oh, did I say that out loud?" Kevin flustered.

"Yes mate. Very out loud."

"Oh, well she said that she's going to pop into the Dragon for a bit tomorrow night, to show a bit of support for her old mutt of a dad. But while she was there she was going to have a chat to us about any possible future business possibilities of a touristic nature, pertaining to that bloody eyesore on the side of your barn," Kevin explained, going all Shakespearean again with the nerves.

"But of course, we're not going to sign up to anything, Glyn, are we now?" Kevin added, "because we've got a plan to put her right off the scent, haven't we!"

Now Glyn was on the wrong foot. Despite telling Kevin that he was going to spend the afternoon working out a well-rounded plan, all that actually happened was that, after he'd been up the bothie to water the plants, he'd been pissing around playing Animal Crossing for a couple of hours until Kevin messaged him to say that he was on his way home. Then he rushed out the front to tape up Banksy's graff and start spraying down the scaffolding. Now it was his turn to come up with something on the hoof.

"Yes!" he said assertively. "Yes we have!"

"Oh good, Glyn," Kevin enthused, "Because my thinking cape is well worn out!"

Glyn gave Kevin his best stare.

"Ohhh, OK, yes, thinking CAP!" said Kevin, hamming it up a bit.

"I reckon that what we do, see, is to tell her flat out that we're not interested! That should see her off!" said Glyn.

"Is that it, butt?" Kevin scoffed. "Even I could have come up with a better plan than that! When that Summer starts on you with her laser beam eyes you'll be agreeing to eat baked toads with frogspawn jam each Christmas if your plan's that poorly developed!"

"Yeah, good point Kev," he replied. "But she just can't flat out make us do something that we don't want to do, can she?"

"Oh I don't know, Glyn. I'm sure she knows hypnosis and that."

"And you know what's bloody worse, Kevin? This means that we've got to go to Bob's poxy barbecue tomorrow. And I don't even like eland! Or at least I'm pretty sure that I don't…"

"But there is some good news," said Kevin, cheerily. "I turned away a load of Banksy spotters down the lane and sent them off to Crosskeys!"

"Kevin, mate. You realise that this is also kind of very bad news as well," Glyn answered, gravely.

"How do you mean, butt?" said Kevin, innocently.

"I mean, yes, it's good that you turned them away – but they were still bloody there, weren't they now. Which must mean that they're on the scent. And if one of them finds it, and it gets out on the internet grapevine, we're bloody buggered man. Might just as well let Summer have her wicked way with us, innit!"

Kevin's eyes widened.

"Not like that, Kev," Glyn laughed. "Not like that."

24

Sunday morning came, and Glyn and Kevin were pottering around the house, trying to work out their best tactics for dealing with Summer later. They thought better of going up the bothie, as on a nice sunny early Autumn day there might have been some hikers about, and they didn't want to draw attention to the produce. The sunshine had also brought out a few more graff hunters to the lanes in their almost exclusive uniform of baggy shorts and bobble hats. But Kevin went out pretending he was on a wander and fed them the now pretty effective Crosskeys red herring, before sending them happily on their way. But there was surely only a few more times that they could pull this trick before someone got wise to their ruse. Glyn thought that the world was slowly closing in on him. He was feeling like a soap bubble on the top of the water in the sink after the plug was pulled out. The nearer it got to the centre, the faster it whizzed round until it was practically a blur, before it got sucked down to the murky depths of the drainpipe below.

After Kevin's latest diversionary foray down the lane, he was up in Glyn's old dad's room, ironing his best shirt.

"What the bloody hell are you running an iron over that tatty old thing for, Kevin you donkey?," Glyn mocked. "It's that Summer, is it? You won't be leaving that barbecue with her on your arm now, I can tell you that for nothing!"

"Ah! No Glyn. It's not because of that!" said Kevin, only lying a little bit. "It's so that we don't go down there all scruffy like, looking like we've just popped in to do a bit of business. If we go down looking like we're making it an afternoon out, no one will suspect us."

"The only thing anyone's going to suspect you of, Kevin, is looking like a right bloody goon!" Glyn laughed. "Just go down in your ordinary clobber, mun. It's only the old Nans who dress up to go to the pub round here these days, anyway. Well, in the daytime at least."

"Well I'm still going to make the effort, Glyn," Kevin asserted.

"Oh go on then, Kevin you old Nan!," Glyn laughed. "You'll make a proper stir you will – one way or another!"

Glyn was right. As the two men walked down to the Dragon, the local feral children on their battered old scooters looked upon Kevin's sartorial choices as an opportunity to resoundingly take the piss.

"Off to court are we, Kevin!" yelled one scrawny lad of about nine in a yellow t-shirt with a half peeled picture in the Ninja Turtles on it, and the remnants of a school holiday mohican sitting scruffily on the top of his head.

"No butt, he's going off to London to visit the Queen!," said another, older lad in a WWE hoodie. "I say, Kevin old chap, do pick me up and OBE and some scones when you're there will you!" he said in an affected regal voice.

Then suddenly, as one voice, the kids began to chant a mocking rhyme to the tune of Big Ben's chimes.

"Shit-shirt Kev-in! Kev-in shit-shirt!" they squealed with delight, as their now clearly rattled quarry hunched his shoulders and shipped on a bit faster past the boys.

"If you don't pull tonight in that shirt, Kevin, I'll snog you myself," shouted one of the boys Nan's from a fold up chair on the little patch of grass in front of her house.

Glyn was beside himself with amusement.

"See, I told you, butt. Rather than blending in with your surroundings, you're looking like a pet peacock on a council estate!"

"Oh shut up, Glyn," Kevin replied in a snap. "No one will be remotely bothered when we get to the pub."

"I hope not, Kevin mate. I bloody hope not," Glyn said, trying his absolute hardest to suppress a guffaw.

As they neared the Green Dragon they could already sense the first few wafts of overheated meat stuffs. As they neared the pub doors, old Jack Evans from up the lane bundled out, sucking his teeth and mopping down the corners of his mouth with an old hanky.

"Oh hello lads! Ooh, what have you come as, Kevin?" said Jack, firing small morsels of bread roll from between his lips like a tiny culinary cannon.

"Oh don't you start, Jack!" Kevin said in a grump.

"Only joshing with you mate! Anyway, bloody lovely, that barbecue is fellas," said Jack. "I must confess, I was a bit dismissive at first, because on the face of it it's a bloody silly idea. But old Bob's just about gotten away with it. It's like a proper barbecue, but with none of that shit smokey smell left on your hair and clothes afterwards. You're going to bloody love it! Anyway, better dash... oh, and try the eland! I haven't got the foggiest what animal it actually is, but it's bloody delicious!"

"It's a kind of big antelope," Kevin proudly announced.

"Ooh, I'll remember that. It's also bloody lovely, that's what it is!," said Jack, still licking his lips.

"Right, enjoy your dinner, and see you up the lane some time!"

"He's right, Kevin," said Glyn. "It does smell bloody nice. But can we be sure that all the meat is actually what he's telling us it is? He's a wily old goat that Bob. For all we know he's been shooting stray dogs and donkeys up on the valley side and he's serving us up that!"

"Ooh, I don't know, Glyn, would he be allowed to do that kind of thing? You know, legally, like?" Kevin pondered.

"Come on, it's Bob we're talking about here, butt," said Glyn. "He just does whatever the bloody hell he wants! And if they are the actual animals he says they are, he's probably just fished them out of the bins round the back of Bristol Zoo – all the diseased ones, like."

"Shut up, Glyn," snapped Kevin, jokily, "You're putting me off my tea!"

They opened the pub doors, and a curtain of misty meat smells wafted over them like a tasty cloud.

"Bloody hell, Kevin butt! If it smells this strong in here, what's it going to be like out back in the skittle alley?"

"I know, Glyn. And it's bloody heaving in here, too. It's going to be absolute carnage back there!"

Both men looked around them at all the pub regulars happily tucking into their exotic afternoon teas. Neither of them could identify what any of it actually was, but it looked bloody tasty. They made their way past the bar, down the short corridor with the toilets and a little half-sized door that nobody had ever really established quite what it was there for, and out into a narrow outdoor lane that led to the skittle bit. There were clouds of savoury smoke billowing out of every crack in the windows and the chatter of much jollity coming from within.

As they burst their way in, they could just about see a row of tables along one side of the skittle alley through the thin blue smoke, each of them laden with a hot and steaming George Foreman grill and a pile of unfamiliar meats to one side, all surrounded by big bottles dripping with a rainbow of colourful condiments. Suddenly they heard Bob's big booming voice cutting through the haze, and he rushed up and clenched the two of them in a big old meat-flavoured bear hug.

"Boys! Boys! So glad you could make it!" Bob roared. "Come in, have some meat!" He lowered his voice and gave a conspiratorial wink. "On the house, of course! It's the least I can do, given the circumstances and all."

"Oh nice one, Bob!" said Kevin. "What's good?"

"Try the ostrich mate," Bob replied. "Bloody lovely it is. Like a cross between beef and turkey, only with some other completely unrecognisably flavour in there too."

"In a good way?" asked Kevin worriedly.

"In a very good way, Kev!" Bob replied. "And how about you, Glyn? What do you want?"

"Ohhhh Bob, well I've heard so much about this bloody eland that I'd better have a go on some of it," Glyn said eagerly.

"Awwww, Glyn mate. We've run out," said Bob sadly. "That Jack from up your lane had the last bit. It was bloody nice though. We couldn't shovel it out of here quick enough."

"Oh man, after all that wondering what it was going to be like and all! I feel almost cheated. What else is good?"

"Well you wouldn't believe it, Glyn lad, but the wildebeest is pretty darned nice. I can see why all them lions go so batshit over it," Bob chuckled.

"Go on then Bob," said Glyn. "Give us a slab of that on a bit of bread then."

"Goes very nice with a dollop of brown sauce," Bob suggested.

"Well there's some words I never thought I'd hear, stood here, in the Green Dragon, in Abertillery," Glyn laughed. "Wildebeest – goes great with a slug of the old HP!"

The three men chuckled as they stood there gnawing on their respective meats – Bob now tucking into a bit of crocodile.

"Didn't go down too well the old croc, mind. The missus reckoned it tasted like tuna-infused carpet tiles, bless her!" Bob laughed. "Ooh, that reminds me, lads. We might have had a spot of good luck here regarding our little, ahem, arrangement."

Glyn and Kevin both leaned in to learn more.

"What's that, Bob?" Glyn asked.

"Well lads, our Elaine, while quite pleasantly surprised at the success of this whole indoor barbecue malarky, didn't want to go off to her Vitulars do stinking quite so strongly of cooked meat. She reckoned she was starting to smell like a burning wildlife park. Anyway, she's off up The Dolls House tonight to see that Judas Priest tribute act with her sister right after we shut the barbecue down."

"I never knew your Elaine was a metal head, Bob?" Glyn said, somewhat surprised.

"Oh she loves her loud and noisy rock music, she does. I think it came from when she used to hang around with those biker gangs in Risca when she was a nipper. She doesn't like to talk about it much, but I think it rubbed off on her musical tastes."

"Well who'd have thought it, eh?!" Glyn responded with a genuine element of surprise in his voice.

"You going up there afters, butt? You could go and say hello to the missus while you're there," asked Bob.

"Oh, I don't know, Bob. It's not really my kind of thing," Glyn explained. "All the bands that play up there have got dumb stupid names like Trigger McPoopshute and Pizza Tramp and The Bay City Roiders, and sing songs about shitting themselves in Tescos and old bollocks like that. Last time I went there was two old English fuckers chucking bogrolls about and making a terrible old racket. Nah mate, I'm much happier sat at home listening to my Hank Williams and my Jimmie Rodgers."

"Each to their own, butt," Bob replied, "although personally I don't go much for any of that noisy old bollocks she likes, either. Anyway, where was I? Oh yes, so she's going up the Dolls with her sister, then they're both going to Linda's pub in Ponty overnight and heading down to Swansea straight from there in the morning. Gives us a whole extra day to get your, ahem, produce down here under the cloak of darkness."

"I'll tell you what, Bob, that's a really beautiful idea," said Glyn. "This place will still be smelling a bit like the Serengeti for a couple of days, and it should mask the sweet smell of bud for a bit while we work out what the bloody hell to do with it."

"Exactly Glyn," said Bob, like some kind of over ripe character from an old black and white Dickensian movie, "Exactly! When do you want to pop it all down?"

"Oooh now, Bob," Glyn asked, "Would it be a stupid question to ask whether we could do it tonight? We've got the council coming round at some point over the next couple of days, you see, and we wouldn't want to surprise them with it. Plus there's some posh New York art gimp coming round Tuesday afternoon. It would make our lives a whole lot easier if we could bring it all down here tonight."

"No problem at all, Glyn," said Bob. "Once we've shifted all this meat and got all these people out of here, we'll probably be closing up early anyway, as we've damn near run out of all the good beer, and no one round here likes any of that craft beer shit. Can't bloody give it away. I'll tidy up a little in here, and then you can start running it all down after midnight. How does that sound to you?"

"That sounds bloody lovely to me, Bob you lightsaber!" said Glyn. "I'd kiss you on your baldy little head if it didn't smell so strongly of charred crocodile."

Kevin, who'd been a little overawed by his ostrich sarnie up to this point looked up from his plate and made a quiet proclamation.

"I tell you what and all, Glyn," he said. "All these George Formbys don't half make it feel warm in here. You'll be able to keep all the produce well nice and toasty if ever there's a frosty night over the next few evenings!"

"George Formbys!" Bob roared. "What are they then? Big banjolele shaped grills that sing A Little Stick Of Blackpool Rock as you char your meat? You great lemon, Kevin!"

"Don't rise to it, Bob," warned Glyn. "It's this thing he does. Just ignore him."

"Actually," offered Bob "banjo or no banjo, the boy's got a very

179

good point. It's lovely and warm in here right now, and it'll keep them little saplings of yours in fine fettle."

"I hate to say it, Bob, but you're right!" laughed Glyn, as Kevin threw him a disappointed side eye.

"Right then Kevin, we're off! Thanks for the wildebeest, Bob! We'll be round a bit later!"

"Cheers fellas," Bob called. "Laters indeed!"

As the pair turned to leave the smoky skittle alley, the door burst open to a fanfare of tiny trumpets as Summer glided in on her very own cloud of pristine silver fog. She was wearing a short, white, Greek style dress with a golden laurel crown on her head, and appeared to be followed everywhere by her own personal wind machine, gently tussling her golden locks about her face as if she was standing on top of some mystical mountain.

Of course, it was only Kevin who actually saw this. To the rest of the skittle alley she was wearing a cosy purple jumper and some jeans that were fashionably torn at the knees. Kevin stood dumbstruck, desperately attempting to rehearse his lines again, but no words would come to him.

"Hello Kevin my love – nice shirt!" Summer said. "You look very dashing! Come here and give me a cwtch!"

Kevin stood awkwardly like a side of old wildebeest while Summer wrapped her arms around him and gave him a little cuddle. He tried to move his arms a little, but she'd got them locked firmly in her bearlike grip, an awful lot like her dad had just done a few moments before.

"Right then, Kevin," she promptly announced, as she finally let the poor fellow get some breath back in his lungs. "Have you told Glyn here about our little plan?"

Both Kevin and Glyn looked at each other with fear written conspicuously across their faces. They appeared trapped, here in this corner of a meat scented skittle alley around the back of a valleys pub, so how in the name of heck were they going to worm their way out of this one?!

25

"Oh hello there Summer," Glyn said, nervously, but still trying to affect some manly bravado "How's it going, butt? Kevin said he saw you in town yesterday. He said something about a bus trip?"

Summer smiled at Kevin, who of course instantly melted, then turned to Glyn and smiled a more hypnotising, mesmeric smile.

"Don't look her in the eye, Glyn," whispered Kevin under his breath. "That way danger lies…"

"That's right, Glyn boy," Summer replied. "We thought you might be interested in having a cut of our action, me and Kevin did. Thought you might like to help out with some of the presentation, like."

"Oh that's not really my kind of thing," Glyn admitted. "But even if I was up for it, we're not in any real position to even think about that right now, if I'm honest with you. We've got the council coming round over the next couple of days to most probably slap a preservation order on the old barn, with a view to getting it listed. So we've got to get it all looking nice and tidy, see. We've got the scaffolding up at the moment – and even if we did have a Banksy on the wall…"

Summer gave him one of her most dangerous, knowing looks.

"…even if we did," he continued, "nobody would be able to see bloody anything for a couple of weeks, anyway. I reckons the council are going to make us renovate the whole damn barn before it would be in any kind of state for people to look at, and that could take us a good three to four weeks at least before anyone could even actually see it. If the weather held out. And if it was even there of course."

Summer looked terribly disappointed at the aching practicality of it all. The tourist footfall always started to slow a bit at this time of year, and this was exactly the kind of boost that her office needed. She wasn't simply going to give up this easily without a fight.

"Oh!" she said, curtly. "Can't you just charge people a quid or two to have a peep behind the curtain, as it were?"

"Well we could," said Glyn, as quick as a flash, "But it would end up taking us twice as long to get the bastard work done, excuse the language. No, I'd rather have it all ship shape and lovely before anyone comes to see it."

Annoyingly Summer could see Glyn's point, even if he had just completely made it up out of his hat.

"Ohhhh, alright then, you little tease," she said, with a resigned look on her face. "You just make sure that you keep me informed about how far the works have gone, then. I've got already got people ringing me up and asking me where the pesky thing is!"

"Well Summer," said Kevin, "if you could just tell them that you've got your spies out trying to find it, and that you'll start arranging trips the minute that you know where it is, that should stall them for a bit. That'll make it sound like you're actively doing something to look for it, too. Wins all round!"

"Kevin love! Summer replied, looking a little surprised at what she'd just heard. "That's actually a really good idea! I'll have to tell everyone in the office to sell the punters that line."

She leaned forward and gave Kevin a quick peck on the cheek and tapped him twice on the shoulders with both hands.

"Right then, have you seen my dad?" she asked.

"Over in the back corner there, hiding in all the meat steam," Kevin answered.

"Oh yes, I see him. Is any of this stuff actually, you know, any good, or is everyone just humouring him?

"Yeah, actually it's all pretty nice," said Glyn. "I'd steer clear of the crocodile, mind, but the wildebeest is bloody lush!"

"Ewwwwww!" Summer replied, her nose all pinched with disgust. "I'm not sure I fancy eating anything with the word beast in its name! I'll see what else he's got. Thanks for the tips, lads. And see you soon, Kevin!"

"Cheers Summer," said Glyn. "We're just off now. We'll keep you posted as to any forward developments."

Summer just nodded, politely, and headed off towards her dad. Kevin swooned a little.

"Shit mun, that was a whole lot easier that I'd feared," Glyn said, somewhat relieved. "Let's get up the bothie and sort out the produce before it gets too dark... Kevin? Kevin mate!"

Kevin was still all moon-eyed as he watched Summer disappear off into a billowing cloud of ostrich smoke.

"She's playing you along, mate," said Glyn, pricking him out of his bedazzlement.

"Yeah, I know Glyn, butt," he wistfully replied. But a boy can but dream. Can we stop off at your house first, mind. I've got to get changed out of this shirt."

Glyn smiled at his dopey mate, and they both headed out of the pub towards home.

26

With Kevin now more suitably attired, he and Glyn hopped onto the quad and headed up towards the bothie. The sheep were acting more normally now – well, at least about as normal as they ever did – so they assumed that the locks on the door had held strong over the last few days. Even Underbite, their favourite old ram, was back to his old familiar tricks of headbutting the trolly and running alongside them like a prancing dressage horse. And when they rounded the the corner to see the bothie all safe and secure and the sheep behaving themselves nice and politely, an eerie feeling began to wash over Glyn.

"I don't like it, Kevin," he said, anxiously.

"What's that Glyn," his pal replied.

"It's all too… too… well too bloody normal, to be honest with you, Kevin. The way things have been going these past few days I was sure we'd turn up here and the bothie would be on fire, or the field would be full off hippies smoked off their tits, or there'd be loads of armed police hiding conspicuously in the woods waiting to pounce. It's all too quiet – I don't like it!

"Or, or…" Kevin added, gleefully "That Barry Scarf Ace sat on a stool in the shed like a gangster in the dark, waiting for us to arrive!"

"Don't be a prat, Kevin lad," Glyn replied. "For a start, you're only adding yet another layer of dark complexity to my already off-the-scale anxiety imagination. And for another, how the bloody hell would he have got into the shed in the first place, but then locked himself in, from the inside? And what did he do? Bring his own bloody stool? He could have been there for days, locked in and sat on his tod, just for the sake of randomly surprising us. Even he's not that warped, surely?"

"That's a very good point there Glyn, and nicely applied," said Kevin. "Although I'm sure he's thought of it!"

Glyn still unbolted the locks with slow, careful trepidation, terrified at the thought of all of the potential nasties that might greet him when he got inside. He slowly opened the heavy, creaky wooden door.

"Well would you bloody well look at that, Kevin!" he cried.

Kevin stopped stock still, in utter fear of what he was about to see as he rounded the corner of the door.

"What's that Glyn?" he asked, quietly, terrified at what Glyn was going to say next.

"Abso-bloody-lutely nothing, Kevin," Glyn said, relieved. "Abso-bloody-lutely nothing at all! Just a whole load of little plants growing happily on their own, without so much as a batchy little mouse nibbling on the stems. How have we been this lucky today with all the bollocks that's been going on around us lately?"

"Ohhhhh tidy darts, Glyn mun," Kevin exhaled. "Let's get them all on the back of the trolley, quick like, before anything untoward does actually happen."

"Good plan, Kevin lad. Good plan!"

The lads had a two-stage strategy to getting all the plants down to The Green Dragon. First of all they'd ferry all the plants down to the old barn, to leave them there for a bit like some kind of a herbal holding bay. Then they'd load the whole lot up onto the back of the old Red Commer truck and shift them down to Bob's under cover of darkness. However, they'd have to give Bob a shout just before they left, just to make sure that Elaine had really gone to stop with her sister. They should be good to leave the stock in the now rather precious barn for a couple of hours, as there were surely no more unexpected visitors likely to be taking a trip up the lane this late in the evening.

The whole operation was running pretty smoothly until the last-but-one run, when in rapidly failing light, the quad hit a big old tree root that was hiding in the long shadows and tipped about half the load out of the back of the trolley.

"Oh bollocks!" Glyn yelped, "Hop off the bike quick and we'll get them loaded back on!"

Halfway across the field, Underbite raised his head and peered into the gloom like some kind of woolly hunting dog. He sensed that something odd was going on down at the bottom of the field, and began to run down and have a look. The boys could hear a strange thundering noise in the distance and looked up to the top of the field, only to see Underbite hammering towards them, seemingly out of control of his own legs.

"Erm, Glyn, is that Underbite up there, hurtling down the hill," Kevin asked.

"You know what, Kev, I think it bloody is!" Glyn answered.

"I think he's gone bonkers for the herb! Quick, get it on the trailer, fast!"

The pair got the last plant on the back of the trailer just as Underbite reached them. But instead of stopping to take a munch out of the precious plants, he kept on running, by now well out of control, and betrayed by his own momentum smashed straight into the wire fence at the bottom of the field. Both lads fell about laughing as the ungainly beast tried to unhitch its entangled horns from the wire, only to get himself into more of a pickle with each backwards thrust.

"The daft bugger was only coming to see what we were doing, bless him," laughed Glyn. "He wasn't trying to nibble our stock, after all!"

"Right then Glyn, let's get him out of that fence," Kevin suggested, humanely.

Kevin grabbed their ovine friend by the horns while Glyn untangled him from the wire.

"Off you go then, Underbite," Glyn yelled as the ram was finally freed from the wire and ran back up the hill, looking a little dazzled.

"Right, that whole unexpected little adventure has set us back a good ten minutes. We'll be hard pushed to get the last lot back down to the barn before nightfall, even if there is only half a load," said Glyn. "Quick, let's get on with it!"

By the time they turned around and got most of the way back up the hill, the coal man of the night time had almost delivered his full load. As it was only going to be a quick run this time, Glyn switched on the quad's lights, but as the pair rounded the last corner again he was filled with horror.

"Fuuuuuck, it's them bloody lampers in our top field, Kev," he huffed. "If PC Alan sees them he's going to come storming up here like the bloody Sweeney, isn't he now."

"No Glyn, we're alright. He won't," said Kevin, confidently.

"How can you be so sure, butt?" Glyn replied.

"Because he's off down Three Cliffs for the weekend with his missus, isn't he, Glyn."

"Oh thank Christ for that," Glyn responded, before swearing quite loudly again. "Bollocks! You know what that mean's not though, don't you Kev?"

"What's that, Glyn?"

"It's only bloody PC Graham taking his place this weekend, isn't it!" Glyn said, with something of a panic on his voice. "And he hates lampers even more than PC Alan does!"

"Oh bollocks Glyn! What are we going to do now?"

"We're going to get these last few plants loaded up and ferried back down the hill and hope that the lampers don't see us and start getting all heavy on our arses," Glyn answered. "If they find out what we've got on the trolly they'll be hassling us for some free samples, and all the while PC Graham will be marching up this hill with his body cam on looking to arrest someone on his last night in the valley."

"You'd better put your foot down then, Glyn," Kevin suggested.

Thankfully the two friends had got up and down the side of the valley with no extra problems and got the produce stashed safely inside the old barn without any of the lampers spotting them while they were about their business. But just as they were about to go back into the house for the keys to the Commer, they heard the crumbling of bicycle wheels coming up the gravelly lane.

"Shit, it's PC Graham," whispered Glyn, "Act normal!"

"I'm not normal though, am I Glyn," his partner in crime replied. "You're always telling me that!"

"Well normal for you…"

"Good evening gentlemen," came a booming voice from the darkness. It was PC Graham.

"We've been having reports that there's been some lamping activities going on somewhere around here," the officer asked in his best serious policeman voice. "You've not seen or heard anything going on, have you now lads?"

"Well actually yes, PC Graham," Kevin suddenly piped up, in that weirdly precise voice that he always used when he was under pressure. "We have. Me and Glyn here were up the top field just now, sorting the sheep out before nightfall, and we could see some flashing and shouting from the next field along. We knew it was lampers, so got out of there pretty quickly, I can tell you. Then, when we got down to the bottom of the hill we could hear them starting to shoot. They really shouldn't be doing that in the dark, officer. They could end up accidentally shooting anyone who happened to be passing by, let alone the damage that they're doing to the local wildlife. I'd get up there and arrest them promptly, officer."

"Well thank you for your kind help, sir," PC Graham replied to the quite unexpected response. "I'd better go and have a word with them right away! What's the best way to get up there without them seeing me?"

"Right, go up this lane to the gate at the end, then turn up the hill and then left when you get to the EU bothie. They're in the field up behind that."

"Nice one, gentlemen, I'll be up there right away," the officer announced, as he skipped onto his bike.

"Oh and one thing, officer," Glyn shouted after PC Graham. "If you get halfway up the hill and you see a ram with a massive underbite charging towards you, don't panic! He's just being friendly, and he won't hurt you!"

"Right you are, lads, I'll keep an eye out!" PC Graham responded as he made his way up the lane.

"Thanks for the help!"

"No worries, sir!" shouted Kevin.

Glyn waited until the locum policeman had gone though the gate, and then turned to his pal.

"Kevin, you're a bloody genius, mate. How did you think of that all by yourself?!"

"Well I was only helping the police out with their enquires, Glyn. What did I do?"

"Right then, so while PC Graham's up there, apprehending those felons, he's not down in the town poking his nose into any of our nocturnal business, is he now," Glyn said, with an exited tone in his voice.

"I suppose not, Glyn boy. Tidy!" Kevin said surprised. "I did good quite by accident!"

"You did, Kevin, you did! Right then, let's use this window of opportunity to load up the Commer, cover the goods up with the old tarp, and get down to Bob's before anyone susses out what we're doing. "For the first time this week, a plan seems like it's actually coming together! Let's go…!"

Perhaps rather surprisingly to all involved, the rest of the operation went without a hitch. Glyn and Kevin laid all the plants onto the back of the Commer's flatbed, latched up the sides and covered the whole lot with the big tarpaulin from the top of the old shed roof. They made it safely down the lane, too. Even remembering the key for the bottom gate. While Kevin was unlocking it, Glyn quickly called Bob to see if the coast was clear – and it was. So they drove cautiously, but not too obviously, down through Cwmtillery and into Abertillery, and pulled up alongside The Green Dragon, up the side lane and off the High Street. They could hear the metal tones of that Judas Priest trib act playing across the other side of town, and knew that they still had a few minutes to finish what they were up to before everyone began to start wandering off home and getting into their business. So they slipped down one side of the flatbed's hinged walls and began to unload, forming a three man human chain as they carried the plants down the side alley and into the skittle shed.

The old brick building was still rich with the smell of charred exotic meats, which masked the more herbal scents of these valuable herbs rather nicely. It was still pretty warm, too, so the plants should quite happily adjust to their new surroundings, the fellas thought.

In the distance, Bob could hear the counterfeit Rob Halford introducing the Priest's old chart hit, Breaking The Law.

"Quick lads, this is their last but one song," he announced. "I reckon we've got a clear ten minutes before have to get a hurry on!"

"How do you know that, Bob butt?," Glyn asked."I thought you hated metal?"

"I do, Glyn lad," Bob answered. "but I've seen this band with Elaine so many times that I know their bloody set off by heart! At least I had a good excuse to get out of it tonight!"

"I feel your pain," Glyn joked, as they grabbed the last few plants off the back of their truck, while the strains of guitar wibbling from the Dolls House floated gracelessly across the Autumn night.

"Right, they're on Living After Midnight now, lads," said Bob. "It's their last song. Let's tidy up and get this alley all locked up. I'm sure they'll end up doing a load of noodling solos at the end, like, so we should still have a bit of time in hand."

The three men put in one last push, and got the doors of the skittle alley locked up safely just as Fakey Halford warbled out the final "Thanks! Goodnight Abergavenny" in a strained falsetto voice.

"Perfect!" said Bob "I'll see you boys in the week then when we've worked out what to do with all that stuff out the back."

"Nice one Bob!" Glyn said as he gave the landlord a hearty handshake. "You've been a true gent!"

"Well, I did owe you one after all after blabbing my mouth all over town about your little artwork, didn't I now. It's the least that I could do!"

"Ooh, Bob, before you go, I have one question," Kevin suddenly called out from the cab of the truck.

"What's that, Kevin butt?" Bob replied.

"What's that Judas Priest tribute lot actually called up there?" Kevin asked. "I know they've always got brilliant, creative names them trib shows, and I'm a little bit fascinated by them."

"Sorry to disappoint you, Kevin lad, but this lot haven't," Bob explained. "They're called Bootleg Priest."

"Well that's a bit shit, isn't it Bob," Kevin replied, all

disappointed. "How terribly unimaginative. It's not even funny."

"Nor are they, Kevin. Nor are they," said Bob with a smile on his face, as Glyn cranked up the Commer and they set off on their way.

The journey back was even less eventful than the journey down, although they did spot PC Graham bundling a couple of lampers into the back of a waiting police van at the bottom of their lanes, which made them even happier. All thing's considered, tonight's operation couldn't have run more sweetly. The lads thought that they deserved an easy night after the last few days of distress, and the whole world of complications that lay ahead of them over the foreseeable future. So when they got back to Daisy Farm, they just parked up the Commer in the garage, slipped an old Sammo Hung DVD into the player, and almost instantly fell asleep on their respective sofas, with a three-quarter-full can of cheap Polish beer grasped precariously in each of their right hands.

27

Kevin was in some kind of Kevin heaven. He was skipping along the long, endless beach at Pendine Sands, the wind in his scruffy mop of hair, and his fingers entwined with those on Summer's tiny graceful hand. The sun was shining, the breaking waves were spraying tiny particles of salty water onto their faces, and they were both wearing floaty white outfits, as though they were the in a video for some terrible holiday pop song. From out of nowhere, the theme music to the sixties war film The Guns Of Navarone started to play loudly, and both Kevin and Summer suddenly looked confused. Summer then began to say Kevin's name over and over again. She sounded irritated, but strangely, each time she spoke she sounded more and more like Glyn.

He blinked twice, and suddenly he was transported back to the sofa in Glyn's living room. Glyn was spraying him with the squirty thing he used to water the houseplants, while his phone was ringing off the hook.

"Wake up Kevin, you daft prat," Glyn laughed. "You must have been having one hell of a dream there lad – you had a right soppy grin on your face!"

Kevin looked sheepish as he continued to wake. "What day is it, butt?" he asked.

"Monday, Kev. It's Monday. Anyway, it's that American bloke ringing again," Glyn continued. "We'd better be up and ready and prepared before we answer it. I'll bung him on speaker phone."

Glyn pressed the green dot of doom, and a loud, brash voice boomed out of the phone.

"Oh Hi! Glyn! André Pinchler here!" said the voice, in a nasal, posh East Coast American accent. "I'm in your beautiful country of Wales Land! And you were soooooo right. As soon as we crossed that funny little bridge everything got so damn quaint and pretty! But I tell you what, I think the guy who painted your road signs got a little drunk, because there's all these random letters just tossed up there! Haha!"

Glyn rolled his eyes in Kevin's direction, then began to speak.

"Oh hello André mate," he said. "How's it going, mun! Where are you now, then?"

"Oh I couldn't begin to tell you how to pronounce all those random letters up on the signs there," the American replied. "But my chauffeur tells me that we're about a half hour away from you. Does that sound good to you?"

Glyn and Kevin both stared at each other and mouthed the word 'chauffeur' with a combined look of puzzlement across their faces. They pictured some kind of long white stretch limo picking its way through the potholes as it drove carefully up the lanes.

"Yeah, no worries, André mate," Glyn replied, cheerily. "We'll have the kettle on, and we've got the biscuits in!"

"Oh!" said André, a little surprised, because biscuits were an entirely different thing where he came from. "OK! Erm, I can't wait! And I can't wait to see that delightful little Banksy on your wall, too, my good fellow. Let's hope that we can come to some kind of, erm, how shall we say it politely… arrangement."

"Let's hope so, André," said Glyn.

"OK, see you in a little while boys. Ciao ciao!" said the American.

"Ciao ciao to you too, André. See you in a bit, now!" replied the Welshman, stifling a giggle at André's art world affectations as he rang off.

"That André's a big bloody posh dollop of a human being, isn't he Glyn," said Kevin, now fully awake after being wrenched so rudely from his slumber, and also trying his best to suppress a chuckle. "I didn't realise that them Americans did posh!"

"Well, them artsy fartsy New Yorker types do, Kev," Glyn explained. "They all pretend like they're so European and cultured, but they just end up sounding like worse twats than the usual rich Americans!"

Both men laughed out loud as they gave the living room a quick tidy up in advance of the impending arrival.

"We don't want that André lad thinking that we live in an old tip now, do we Kevin!" Glyn laughed. "And anyway, what were you dreaming about before I woke you up? You looked proper happy you did. Proper happy!"

"Oh, I dunno, Glyn butt. I can't remember," said Kevin. "I can never remember my dreams," he added, knowing full well that he could recall every last glorious second of it.

About forty five minutes later the boys could hear what sounded like a vehicle of some substantial size coming up the lane, and some loud chamber music was floating through the trees alongside it. They raced out to the front of the house to see a big black limo picking its way through the potholes, just as they'd imagined. Only this was a more standard length model rather than one of those stretch affairs that the girls from Cardiff always rented out for their hen nights.

"Hold on a minute," Glyn suddenly said, a bit startled. "How the bloody hell did they get up here? I thought the gate was locked? Did you remember to lock it last night? I don't want any other freaks driving up here today!"

"Ooh, I'm not sure," said Kevin. "I'm pretty sure that I hopped out and did it on the way back last night."

"Well you better had have done!" Glyn answered, crossly.

After a long struggle up the lane, the limo finally pulled up outside Daisy Farm, and a tall, slim figure in a sharp black Italian suit and a white open-necked shirt got out. Now this wasn't what Glyn and Kevin had imagined at all. They'd half expected some guy in a big white fur coat carrying a small startled dog in a Gucci backpack. But no, this chap looked almost serious and businesslike.

"Guys guys, it's so good to finally meet you!" the American bellowed. "And what a journey that was. We didn't think we'd find you. Especially after some ruffians in the last town started to throw rocks and sticks at the car!"

Glyn and Kevin looked at each other with a smile, as they knew exactly who those ruffians were likely to be.

"And you were so right," the American continued. "We met the most charming British bobby who unlocked the gate for us and gave us the final directions. Do you have your own security now?"

"Ahhh, PC Alan's back from Three Cliffs, isn't he now," said Glyn under his breath.

"Thank goodness for that, said Kevin. "I was beginning to doubt myself!"

"So!" The American announced, all businesslike. "Let's have a look at the merchandise shall we!"

The lads led André up to the scaffolding, and began to unravel the netting.

"We've had to cover it up and protect it, André lad," Glyn explained. "We didn't want people coming up and vandalising it before we'd had a chance to talk to you. And that Team Robbo have been up here causing trouble, too. So we thought it better to be safe than sorry."

"Good thing too!" the American proclaimed, in a slightly patronising manner, annunciating each word as if it was a separate sentence. "Terrible art hating heathens, that they are! You did well to cover it up in time."

Glyn helped the American up onto the scaffolding and began to peel back the plastic that he'd taped over the graffiti.

"Here you go, André, an exclusive viewing," Glyn proudly announced. "The latest Banksy! You're probably only the sixth or seventh person to ever see it!"

"I feel highly honoured, Glyn," said the American, before cutting himself dead in his tracks.

"Oh! Is that it?" the American said, sounding more than a little disappointed. "I just assumed that Banksy's own Instagram post had understated it a little. But there's really not much to it, is there!"

"True enough," said Kevin. "But how many unfinished Banksy works have you ever seen around the world?"

"Well none, I must confess," said André, a little impressed at Kevin's moxy.

"And added to that," Kevin continued, "we can tell the full story behind it – the provenance if you will – and can show you the messages that the lad himself sent us to apologise for turning our lives into such a big unruly mess!"

"Oh how utterly delightful," said the American as he clapped his hands together once in an expression of glee! "You've got such a good story behind it all, despite it looking so ugly and unfinished. And seeing as, the lad himself, as you so charmingly put it, has admitted to the whole thing, I reckon I could easily find a buyer for it. Obviously it's not as iconic as many of his other pieces, and I can't see this ending up on the side of any mugs or tote bags, so it doesn't have that sell on effect – which is going to trouble the price we get a little, of course. So we could maybe get you in the range of about one-fifty for it."

"A hundred and fifty thousand pounds was that, André," Glyn enquired.

"Dollars, dear boy. Dollars," the dealer replied. "The art market works strictly in American money."

"Oh, I have to say that… not being greedy like… but we were expecting something a little bit higher than that," Glyn replied, the disappointment barely hidden in his voice.

"That's still good value though for a few old bricks and a couple of flicks of paint, Glyn sir," the American countered. "And that's also the profit that you'll get once we've taken out all the costs of taking the bricks out of the wall, shipping it to America, and all the auction fees and everything – my own tiny little cut included. That's still a pretty tidy sum for something this incomplete."

"Fair point, André," Glyn reasoned. "I never really thought about all that extra stuff. And I reckon it's still a pretty decent amount of money for, like you say, a few old bricks."

"Exactly, Glyn sir! Exactly!" The American enthused.

"Erm, Glyn mate," Kevin whispered into the back of his friend's head. "What about the council?"
"Oh bollocks," said Glyn worriedly. "I'd forgotten all about them!"

He turned back to the American with a serious look on his face.

"There might be one, small, problem about taking the old stone blocks out of the wall and shipping them out of the country, André."

"Oh really, Glyn?" said the American, now looking a bit serious himself. "Do tell!"

"Well apparently these barns are a really rare kind of structure that are unique to this valley, and the local council are looking to slap a preservation order on them – which will mean that if we do take any of the bricks out, we could be left facing a pretty hefty fine at the end of it all, and probably left with a big bill to fix up any holes that the extraction leaves," Glyn explained.

"Oh!" said the American. "That might be a bit of a problem. I'm sure that we can smooth it all over with your local authorities though. The barn doesn't look all that old though. What is it, a hundred years or so?"

"It's probably older than your country, André," said Kevin.

"What, 1776 and all that?" the American laughed.

"No mate, before Christopher Columbus and John Cabot started going over there and annoying the locals and giving them diseases," Kevin continued. "Centuries old these are, butt."
"Oh!" said the American, now looking a little concerned. "Yes, that is terribly old. Practically prehistoric! I guess we could ship the whole damn barn over as some kind of concept piece though?"

"We'd want a lot more money than a ton-fifty for that though, André mate," said Glyn, with his steeliest business glare on. "A whole lot more. I mean, just think of the inconvenience."

"Yes, I can quite understand your position there, Glyn," the American reasoned. "I'll have to go back and talk to my people about it. There may be a little bit of monetary wiggle room that we can arrange. I won't write you a cheque just now then. But I'll call you with a potentially revised offer when I get back to NYC. Does that sound good to you, Glyn?"

"That'll do me for now," came Glyn's stoic reply.

Just as the American was getting back into his limo, Kevin noticed something out of the corner of his eye down at the bottom of the lane.

"What's all that commotion down there, Glyn mun," he asked puzzled.

"I dunno, Kevin butt," Glyn replied. "I can see some kind of a light, and some bloke dressed in black beetling about, and someone holding a long pole with... a long furry thing on, I think?"

"Hang on a minute..." said Kevin. "You know who that bloody is, don't you?"
"No idea, Kevin mate. But I think you're about to tell me."

"It's that Polish art bloke off the telly. Well not Polish, but he's got a Polish name," Kevin burbled.

"I dunno who you mean, Kevin mate."

"Oh you know, Voldemort Jankychank, or something like that... You know, off BBC4!"

"Oh, I know the one you mean," said Glyn, finally translating what Kevin was actually on about. "That big boisterous bloke who's always marching about in some foreign city, pointing at stuff. I usually hate all those arts doccos with posh people just wistfully walking about in Paris and Florence. Why do they always walk about so bloody much? At least this Voldemort bloke usually has a purpose to his stamping around. He's always actually going somewhere!"

Glyn stopped his chatter for a moment, and looked puzzled.

"And more to the point," he continued after a moment, "What the bloody hell is he doing up our lane with a camera crew in tow?"

André looked up, stared down the lane, and bellowed out a hearty roar.

"Waldemar? Waldemar dear boy! You made it I see!"

"Wait! What?" Glyn said, by now a little miffed at everything that was going on in front of him. "You actually invited my favourite art bloke off the telly, whose name I am still utterly unable to say..."

"Waldemar Januszczak?" said André.

"Yeah, that's the one," Glyn agreed, " So you asked this Waldemar bloke up to our house to put us in one of his films, and you didn't think to ask us?"

"Oh Glyn dear, I thought you'd be delighted! Are you not?" the American exclaimed. "Waldemar's an old friend of mine, and I bumped into him at the Tate yesterday. He told me that the BBC had commissioned him to do a series about the history of street art, and I let him in on our little secret. He just jumped at the chance of getting a never-before-seen piece of Banksy's work in his film before the whole world got to find out about it, and I thought you'd love it too. And you know what? It may even raise the value of your old barn wall by a few of your English quids…"

"You really should have checked in with us first though, André," said Glyn, by now utterly exasperated. "We're just not ready for this level of attention, to be honest with you, mate…"

"Well get ready for it, Glyn, because your life's never going to be the same again," said the American, with a bold extravagance in his voice.

"That's just it, see André," said Glyn, plaintively. "I'm rather happy with my quiet little life. I want my life to be the same. I don't want to see my face plastered all over the telly and the papers. I just want get on with what I was up to a week or two back, but the whole bloody thing's just got so bloody surreal, mate."

"No it hasn't, Glyn," Kevin suddenly piped up.

"How do you mean, butt?" Glyn asked his mate, a little confused.

"It's not surreal, Glyn," he explained. "Surrealism is an art movement whereby two or more disparate objects or concepts are juxtaposed to make their own, often dreamlike artistic scenario. What's happening to you is unreal. Unlikely. Quite unexpected at best. I bloody hate it when people on the local news have something only vaguely remarkable happen to them and they always bleat out about how bloody surreal they think it is. No mate. It's not. Winning that Olympic qualifying boat race isn't surreal. It's unlikely. And exciting. But it's not bloody surreal. If it was surreal you've have rowed a bloody Welsh Dresser across a sea of peas wearing a purple bowler hat. So this is unreal, Glyn, not surreal. You're always picking on me for the way I say things, but this one has always got right up my arse!"

"Ohhhh, sorry Kevin, mun, I didn't think," Glyn answered, sheepishly. "You da watch too many of those art documentaries, mind."

The American, however, looked impressed. "Kevin young man, you certainly do know your stuff," he said. "We'll make an art critic out of you yet, good sir!"

"Oh cheers, butt! Nice of you to say so," Kevin answered, a little bewildered.

By this point, Waldemar Januszczak had worked his way up the lane, skittering from side to side, constantly looking over his shoulder and talking to the camera that a poor operator had been holding in a low stoop below his knees.

"Hello chaps!" the TV art critic said with a familiar avuncular

208

tone. "I understand that you've got a Banksy. Do you mind if we have a look at it?"

Glyn wasn't so sure. "Hello there, Waldemar mate," he said. "It's a pleasure to actually meet you in the flesh…"

"And yourself sir," the art critic responded. "André here's told me all sorts about you."

"He has?" said Glyn, surprised. "Any road, do you mind turning the cameras off for a minute and having a proper chat first. We've got a few complications, see."

"That's quite alright, mate," the art critic agreed. "Cut lads, cut!" He gestured towards his crew using a cut throat gesture with his right hand, and the two men sat down. The cameraman especially looked glad of a few minutes rest.

"So what's the problem here, exactly, chaps?" Waldemar asked in a friendly manner.

"Well to be honest with you, Waldemar – if I can call you that?" Glyn asked.

"Glyn sir, if you can say it, you can call me it!" the art critic said, cheerily. " I get called all sorts, I can tell you – Voldemort most of the time. So I appreciate you going to the trouble of getting it right. Anyway, you were saying…?"
"Oh. Cool. OK. Well to be honest with you mate, we're not exactly cut out for all this televisual lark. We're just two quiet lads from South Wales who want to mind our own business and get on with our lives. All this Banksy business has made things

terribly complicated," Glyn explained. "And what's more, if the local council slap a preservation order on us by the end of the day we'll have no choice in the matter, and our lives are going to become a bloody three ring circus with all them graffiti fans wandering up and down the lane at all hours, every day of the week, aren't they now."

Waldemar Januszczak looked genuinely moved at the poor fellow's predicament.

"I quite understand, Glyn," said the art critic, his ruptured vowels now full of calm understanding. "I don't think that Banksy lad quite realises the trail of mayhem that he leaves behind him, does he! I'll tell you what. Do you mind if we just go and have a look? If we can get the angles right we'll film it in close up so that nobody can identify quite which building it's on. And then I'll give a bit of bunkum on the telly about secret locations and all that guff, and shoot some general views somewhere else further down the valley to put people off the scent. That way, by the time my film comes out, nobody should be able to work out where it's actually located. How does that sound to you, chaps?"

"That sounds like just about the nicest, kindest thing that anybody has done for us in over a week now," Glyn said, all relieved. "Thank you Waldemar mate."

"Don't mention it Glyn," the art critic replied humbly. "Now let's go and have a look at it, shall we?"
"Prepare yourself for disappointment though, Val!" André said in his big, booming voice. "It's not perhaps the artist's best work."

Glyn helped Waldemar up onto the scaffolding and peeled back the protective plastic.

"Ah yes, I see what you mean André. It looks a little... incomplete."

Kevin whispered to Glyn "He talks just like he does on the telly, butt."

"Shhh, I'm listening," Glyn whispered back. "This piece of critique might bag us a few extra quid when it comes to auction time!"

"Can you roll the camera again, lads of the crew?" Waldemar asked his weary sidemen. "I've got a piece to camera brewing."

The camera operator and the sound recordist rose to their feet, picked up their gear and walked towards the scaffolding.

"Right chaps, be sure not to get any actual scenery in, and make it look like I'm uncovering this old bit of tat for the first time. Are we ready?"

"Yes Val," said the camera operator. "In three, two, one... rolling."

The art critic instantly clicked into TV mode. He swung up the scaffolding like a tradesman, uttering fragments of artsy sounding statements as he did.
"...and here... if I just peel back this bit of protective plastic... that's been been put here to protect it from miscreants and foul deeds... you'll see... a very ordinary bit of stencil work... from an otherwise grand master of the street arts..."

He paused for a moment, just staring at the paintwork, before yelling "And cut!"

"Cheers chaps," he said in his now-familiar friendly manner. "I'll fill in the rest of the narrative in voice over. Can you just give me a little bit of context though? Do you happen to know why it's unfinished?"

"Well we chased the little bastard off, didn't we Glyn," said Kevin.

Waldemar looked instantly delighted at this tale. "Stop, stop just a moment. Do you mind if I record you telling me this? It sounds like terrific stuff. We won't film you though. Well just get the sound and then retell your story."

"Well as long as nobody knows that it's us?" Glyn asked, warily.

"They won't, they won't, trust me. Now, are you rolling, Michele?" he asked his sound operator.

"Yep, rolling!" came the reply.

"So chaps, tell me all that again," Waldemar asked, "why didn't that Banksy fellow finish this particular piece of work?"
"Well, we chased the little bastard off, didn't we now," repeated Kevin.
"Yeah, butt," Glyn continued. "We just thought it was some little tagging shitbag from down the valley. But then when he nearly fell off his ladder we could see that he was some old bloke with glasses."

"Yes, and then we chased him off with a pitchfork and a water pistol full of chilli seeds," added Kevin. "You've never seen a bloke in such a blind panic before! Quite literally blind after the chilli got him in the eye!"

"Excellent stuff, chaps!" the art critic enthused. "I can use all of this! Now, did you take a good look at him? Enough to be able to tell who he, or indeed, she was?"

"Well, like we said, it was definitely a bloke, and he was much older than us, had glasses, and just looked like a normal geezer, really," said Kevin.

"So it definitely wasn't the fella from Massive Attack then?" asked Waldemar.

"Oh no," said Kevin, "I've seen him out and about, and he's definitely not that funny."

"Yes, I've heard that," Waldemar agreed. "The other rumour I've been hearing is that it's Jimmy Cauty from the KLF. Do you think it could have been him?"

"Who's that then?" asked Glyn.

"You know, one of them blokes who had all them pop hits in the charts, but then got bored with it all and burned a million quid on some Scottish island," Kevin explained.
"Oh that pair of wasteful bastards!" Glyn angrily countered. "We could have done with some of that money around here back in the nineties, I can tell you. Is he from Bristol?"

"Well I don't know where he lives now," said Waldemar, "but

I'm pretty sure that he's from somewhere up north originally.

"Oh this bloke definitely had a big dollop of fruity West Country corners in his voice," said Glyn. "So I don't think it's that KLF bloke."

"This is all brilliant context, gentlemen," Waldemar enthused. "You've helped us out tremendously. Thank you so much. Cut Michele, cut! Right, we'll be off then. I think we've got everything we need here. Could you possibly give us a lift back down to the bottom of the hill, André, when you're done sir?"

"Oh, I think I'm done here now Val," said the American. "Look, guys, we're still on for this, right? Right! I'll give you a call when I get back to New York and we'll see what we can work out. I'm pretty sure that we can make this a worthwhile outcome for everyone involved. See you now. Ciao ciao!"

"Ciao ciao!" the two Welsh lads said in unison, now almost as a reflex.

As Waldemar Januszczak was about to jump into the car, he stopped and yelled out to Glyn and Kevin.

"You pair have been a tremendous help, today. If there's anything else I can do to help you, here's my card. If you need to know something, anything, just give me a call."
Then he leaned out of the window a bit further towards the couple and whispered, conspiratorially. "And if he offers you any kind of deal," he said, gesturing towards André, "run it by me first. He's a mate and all, but he'll always try to get the minimum possible deal out of you!"

"Cheers Waldemar!" the pair said happily. And with that he was in the car. The long limousine started up, and ticked over for about a minute, before it stopped again and the chauffeur hopped out, looking puzzled.

"Erm lads," he asked. "I'm not entirely sure how I'm going to get out of here. It's going to be a right pain backing it out down all these pits and potholes. Is there any way to turn round up ahead?"

"Yes mate," Glyn answered. "You can turn it around in the field up ahead. I'll just run up there and open the gate."

"Awww thanks mate," said the driver in a proper working class London accent. "You're a true gent!"

And with that, the massive car rolled carefully up the lane, drove through the now opened gate, and cut a massive arc around the heavily sloping field.

"Terrible turning circle these big buggers have got!" the driver joked out of the window, before he straightened up and started to head on down the lane.

"Cheers mate!" the driver yelled, as Waldemar Januszczak and the New York art dealer waved at them out of the open side windows.
"Well Kevin," said Glyn. "Have we ever had a stranger, more utterly batshit hour of our lives than what just happened there, now?

"No!" said Kevin with a knowing smirk. "One could almost say that it was quite surreal!"

Glyn batted his pal friendlily across the top of his head, and just as they were walking back to the cottage, felt his phone throbbing in his pocket. He pulled the phone out to see that he was being alerted to an voicemail, and quickly pressed the button to call his inbox.

"I'd better get this voicemail, Kevin butt," he said. "The way things are going these days you never know who it's likely to be. I'm half expecting it to be Graham Norton on the end of the phone, eh!"

He listened for a moment and went visibly grey.

"Oh bollocks, Kevin," he said with fear in his eyes. "It's the bloody council…"

28

Glyn started the message again and tapped it onto speakerphone so that Kevin could hear.

"Hello yes, sorry we missed you. This is the council here, with regard to the planned visit to your barn. Unfortunately our chief listing inspector has gone down with a bad case of food poisoning, and will be unable to start their inspections today. The process is expected to begin again on Tuesday. However, we would just like to reiterate that any clear and obvious recent damage to these buildings may result in a compulsory purchase order from the council, as well as strict listing restrictions being imposed upon said buildings. I'm sure that this won't be the case in your instance, but I felt it only fair to inform you of this matter in advance, so that there won't be any nasty surprises down the line. Oh, and if you need to call me for clarification on any of these matters, my name's Ros Llewellyn, and you can get me via the number that I've just called from. Thanks for listening. Goodbye!"

"Well she sounded a bit bloody stern, Glyn," Kevin said as he looked up from the phone.

"I know, butt," Glyn replied. "And I didn't like all that business about compulsory purchase orders. Them buggers at the council are looking for any excuse to pay us well below the going rate, then to pack that whole barn up and take it down St Fagans outdoors museum to put alongside all those Miners Institutes and dead pubs and tanneries that they've got there. And I reckon they're thinking that if they've got a Banksy bunged on the side of it they're going to get a whole load of extra people coming in through their gates that they otherwise wouldn't have got. We can't risk it, Kev. We can't give them the excuse they're bursting for to nick our old barn!"

"Bit of luck about the food poisoning thing though, Glyn," said Kevin. "Do you think they had the crocodile down at Bob's barbecue last night?"

"Ha, it wouldn't surprise me in the slightest," Glyn laughed. "I can see why everybody steered clear of it – it smelled bloody rank! What this also does though, Kevin, is give us another day's leeway to come up with some scheme to get out of this bloody great hole this shit bit of graffiti's got us into. I really don't know what we'll be able to do about it, to be honest with you..."

At that moment Glyn's phone rang again, and the cloud of sadness that was beginning to envelope his face turned to one of mild annoyance.

"It's that bloody Bob again!" he huffed."What the bloody hell does he want now?"

He answered the phone. "Yes Bob, hello. What's up?"

"Hello Glyn my old darling," Bob's loud voice boomed, half deafening Glyn, who'd clean forgotten that he'd left his phone on loud speaker mode after the last call. "How's it going?"

"Yeah Bob," said Glyn, slightly distracted as he scratched his now muffled right ear. "What's happening?"

"Well I've got some good news and some bad news regarding the merchandise, Glyn," the landlord explained.

"That's all I need, some more bloody bad news, Bob," Glyn huffed. "So we'd better start with that to get it out of the way, eh!"

"Alright Glyn," Bob agreed. "It's not all THAT bad, anyway. Just a little bit annoying."

"Go on…"

"So, while I was cleaning up the skittle alley last night, I'd thought I'd give it a little dry run at warming up the plants with the George Foremans…"

"I'm already not liking the sound of this, Bob, but go on," said Glyn with a worry in his voice.

"Well, two things happened really," sad Bob. "The first thing was that if I got them too close to the actual plants, the edges began to curl up a little bit…"

"Oh Bob you absolute tool!" snapped Glyn.

"But don't worry. Only a couple of plants got damaged, and they're still looking pretty green and vibrant."

"I'll take your word for it, Bob," Glyn said, rolling his eyes. "What's the other bad thing then?"

"Well, it got so warm in the alley that the plants started to let out this rich, sweet skunk-like aroma that started to waft out into the pub," said Bob. "It was bloody lovely, mind. But I'm not sure I can be doing with that all the time, see. The old bill will be on it in an instant, won't they now."

"That's actually a very good point, Bob," said Glyn, sounding relieved. "And for once your bad news wasn't actually that bad. So thanks for checking that out for us – but be careful with the little blighters in the future, right."

"Oh I will, Glyn butt. I will," Bob replied. "So! Do you want the good news now?"

"I suppose now is as good a time as ever, Bob."

"Well, you know how my brother-in-law – you know, Elaine's twin – is always looking for a new get rich quick scheme," Bob whispered.

"I know the fella, Bob," said Glyn. "And I never realised that him and Elaine were twins! I always thought he was much older than her?"

"He's actually 13 minutes younger, would you believe it. But that's all another story for another day, Glyn mun," Bob teased. "Anyways, he was helping me clear up in the pub after the indoor barbecue, and noticed the mild waft coming from out the back. Of course, you know me, I couldn't keep my gob shut, so I showed him the plants, and now he wants to buy them off you to start up his own operation over in New Tredegar."

Glyn's brain began to roll like the wheels in a fruit machine, and it took a couple of sticks and nudges before the value of this plan began to sound like a good idea. And he had to confess, it would get him out of at least a couple of the deep holes he'd found himself in.

"You know what, Bob?" Glyn said when the wheels all eventually clicked into place, five bells in a row. "Normally I'd think that would be a rotten plan. But right now, in the position we're in, that could actually work to our favour. What's he offering?

"Well he reckoned twenty five K, Glyn butt. Fifteen up front, with another ten after he'd made a bit of money off it."

Glyn began to work out the potentials of this little deal in his mental notebook. Fair enough, it was a bit less than it was worth, and a fair bit less than Scarf Ace offered him. But of course, he'd lost a chunk of stock to that unwelcome sheep invasion, and New Tredegar was just far enough away to be off his localised patch, and shouldn't really cause him any loss of business. And more importantly, it was also far enough away not to be of any immediate concern to Scarf Ace. Twenty five K still sounded a little light for what it was actually potentially worth, though, so Glyn made a counter offer.

"I can't do it for that low, Bob butt," he haggled. "How's he fixed for giving me thirty five?"

"He told me that thirty was the highest he could go," said Bob cagily.

"Call it thirty one and I'll chuck in some specialised fertiliser, Bob," Glyn cheekily asked.

"Done, Glyn mate. Done," Bob laughed.

"I think I have been, Bob mate. Let him know that I'm only

221

selling it to him on one cast iron condition, though," Glyn added, gravely.

"Ooh, what's that Glyn boy?" said Bob.

"That he must never, ever, on any circumstances, tell that Scarf Ace fella where he got it all from, right!"

"Understood Glyn mate. Very much understood."

"If anyone ever asks, get him to tell them that he grew them from seed that he got sent over from America on the internet," Glyn suggested. "Our names must absolutely never be involved in this transaction after he's paid us the cash!"

"Bang on, Glyn. I'll make sure of it," Bob agreed. "And on a similar tip, our Elaine must never know that I acted as the middle man on this deal… or that I ever even had the plants in the pub."

"That sounds like a reasonable trade off, Bob! Let's virtually shake on it!"

"Right you are, Glyn lad," said Bob, quite proud of himself at the deal he'd just brokered. "I'll give him a shout now, and you can expect the first wedge of cash by Wednesday."

"Can he stretch to sixteen on the first instalment, Bob," Glyn asked. "Our overheads have started to get understandably a bit high over the last week or so."

"I'll ask him, Glyn boy. And I can't see why ever not. I'll bung him the extra grand myself if it's an issue."

"You're a good man, Bob," said Glyn. "It's not true what everybody says!"

"Why you cheeky bastard Glyn!" Bob snuffled. "Right, I'm off to break him the good news. Talk later in the week, mate."

"Right you are, Bob!"

As Glyn rang off, you could see the blood slowly beginning to pour back into his face.

"Absolute bloody result," he said, punching the air like a tennis player. "That's taken one fuck-ton of weight off my shoulders for the day. Now we've just got to worry about the other fuck-ton painted on the side of my old barn."

"Bloody good job of haggling there, too Glyn," Kevin said, impressed at his pal's work on the phone.

"I mean, it's less than it's worth, but to be honest with you, at the moment I don't give all that much of a shit, and it's one less thing to give us grief. Mind you, what's all that commotion down the bottom of the lane?"

Obviously, having a limo and a TV crew moogling about wasn't an every day occurrence around these parts, and the local kids were starting to come up for a nose about.

"Oh that's the last bloody thing we need, right now, Kev," said Glyn with his grumbly face glued firmly back on. "See if you can get down there and tell them to piss off in your usual diplomatic style, butty. I reckon I'd deck one of them if I went down to confront them right now, I'm in such a dark mood. And you never quite know who their dads are, either."

"Neither do they, Glyn," Kevin laughed, "Neither do they!"

"Oooh, harsh, Kev mun!" Glyn winced. "Just see if you can shift them politely on. And if you can't, I'll drive the Commer at them!"

"Ha, alright Boutros Boutros-Ghali!" Kevin chuckled. "I'll get down and see them off!"

Kevin walked down the lane towards the kids with a friendly look on his face. "Alright chaps, what are you lot doing up here?"

"Hey look, it's Shit-Shirt Kevin!" said one especially urchin-like lad, and the rest of the kids began to laugh, chanting "Shit-Shirt! Shit-Shirt!" as he approached.

"Yes yes, very funny chaps," Kevin said sweetly, trying to resist stamping down really hard on the ringleader's toes. "But what brings you up here? We don't often see you so far out of town."

"Well Shit-Shirt," the lead urchin mocked, "We sees that limo driving round the lanes, and then that film crew that followed them, so we thought there must have been some kind of Hollywood film being, erm, filmed up here. So who is it then? George Clooney? Brad Pitt? Iron Man? Tell us it's a bloody Marvel film, Kev, then we can be in it!"

Kevin pondered for a moment while he made up his excuse, but he figured he'd rustled up a good one.

"To be absolutely honest with you, they'd come to the wrong place," he bumbled. "They'd been looking for that new Banksy down in Crosskeys, but they took the wrong turn and came up the valley."

The lead urchin looked like he wasn't prepared to take this kind of unlikely nonsense, and grilled Kevin further.

"No disrespect, Kev, but that sounds like a shit excuse," he scoffed. "So why were they up here for so long then?"

The lad clearly didn't believe a word he was saying, but quick as a flash Kevin mustered up a pretty believable answer.

"Well have you ever tried to turn a limo around up a narrow country lane?" he suggested, now a little more confident. "Took them bloody ages, didn't it now. That driver must have done a fifty point turn to get it out."

The lead urchin looked defeated, and scrunched up his face in annoyance.

"Yeah, good point, Kev," he conceded. "I'll buy that. But if we see them up around here again we'll be up your house like a shot!"

"Don't worry, you won't," Kevin added. "They're long gone. See you then, young'uns!"

"Yeah, see you Shit-Shirt!" the kids shouted, before running back off down the lane, chucking rocks at each other and whacking the smaller kids with massive sticks, as kids in clusters tend to feel compelled to do.

"Well that was far easier than I'd anticipated," Kevin said to himself as he walked back up to Daisy Farm with a spring in his step. "Things seem to be finally going our way today!"

But as he reached the cottage he saw Glyn talking urgently down the phone, before ringing off and chucking his device into a bush.

"What's up, Glyn, butt?" Kevin asked. "What's got you so angry now?"

"It's the press, Kevin. They're bloody onto us."

29

Kevin looked concerned at Glyn's news.

"What, the bloody tabloids," he fretted. "I don't want my face going in all them shitwipe rags!"

"Not yet, Kevin," Glyn assured him."It was only the local Gazette. But once it's in there it'll get everywhere, and we'll be having journos and TV crews from all over popping up for a chat."

"So what did they say, Glyn?"

"Well this reporter piped up, all chirpy like – 'Hello, I believe that you have a Banksy on your wall, and we'd love to come over and have a little chat about it, maybe take some pics as well. What time are you free over the next couple of days?' All that kind of thing. I told them that it wasn't on my old barn, but I'm pretty sure that she didn't believe a word of it. That's it, Kevin butt. Once it's in one paper it'll spread like a disease, and the whole bloody planet will know where we are. We'll be marked on Google Street View, Summer will be running her bus trips, and we'll just be sat here like lemons waiting for it all to go away. But it won't. Them buggers are still shuffling into the Sistine Chapel five hundred years after that Michael whatsit bloke painted his roof thing up there, ain't they."

Kevin laughed at his pal. "Yes, but it's not quite the same though, is it," he said, trying to comfort his pal. "That's a work of great artistic value that took him bloody years to complete, and is dedicated to God's great glory, if you believe all that nonsense.

All we've got here is a half-finished picture of Thatcher with her shit face on that took the artist a good five minutes to fuck up. And even he thinks it's rubbish!"

"I get your point, Kevin, I really do, and thanks for trying to cheer me up," answered Glyn, dolefully. "But they'll still all want to come and have a look, won't they. The art critics and the graffiti fans and the passing strangers who want to know what all the fuss is about – and the local kids! They'll be the bloody worst. They'll be tagging the rest of the wall, asking the visitors for fags and spare change, and chucking rocks at my sheep before we know it. I mean, just look at how many people have been up here trying to have a piece of us since that bloody thing went up! And all of them have been some level of unhinged. I just can't be doing with that magnitude of nonsense going on in my life, to be honest with you. In the last week or so we've chased an internationally renowned artist off our property with pitchforks and water pistols, had serious threats from both a local drug lord and the local council – and I'm not sure which is the worst! We've had the old bill round, who apparently know all about our every move in the local pharmaceutical trade. Then there's been your Summer and her tourist information mob who want to send their bloody bus trips up here, we've had American art knobs trying to buy our back wall, that Waldemar off the telly filming our back wall, all manner of dopy waifs and strays wandering around looking for art's holy grail, not to mention those threats from them poxy London art terrorist wannabies. And all that's before the local press have come sniffing round... and not even taking into account the many, many miles our poor little plants have travelled around the valley in the last few bloody days! That's it. I'm done. I'm not built for this kind of stress and hassle. It's coming off! I don't care how much it's worth on the open market. If old André starts coming down here with his extraction crew we'll lose the barn to the local council anyways, and then all the art fans will come and start bricking my windows for even daring to move one of their darling bloody bits of graff away from its natural home, Kevin, butt. We'll get the shit end of the stick whatever we end up doing, so we might just as well pretend that the whole thing never happened. That old boy down in Port Talbot was right, the poor sod – this whole thing has been a poisoned chalice from start to finish, and I'm beginning to understand why he got shot of it so quickly now! And anyway, that Banksy lad said that he was going to send us something to make up for the hassle anyway, so we'll probably get a bob or two from that if he gives us one of his squiggles or dollops. So I reckon we should just bust our flush, scrub the fucking thing off and then just get back to normal. Who'd have thought that bloody Margaret Thatcher would be causing me so much bloody aggravation even to this day! I used to hate the wizened old claw-handed crone before. I can't tell you how much pleasure it would give me to scrape her horrible face off the barn now."

"But Glyn mate, wait a moment and think about it," Kevin interrupted, trying to talk his mate out of such a rash decision. "A hundred-and-fifty grand is a lot of money for anyone around here. Just think of all the things you could do with it. You could go to Nashville like you've always wanted to."

"It's a big old lump of money, I can't deny Kev," Glyn said, "But I really can't be doing with the hassle any more. My head's been fizzing all week, and this is just the easy bit at the start! I'm utterly fed up with this whole ridiculous charabanc of shit. Nah mate, my mind's made up, it's coming off right now! Go fetch the wire wool from the shed, and I'll get the whitewash out!"

Upon Kevin's return, Glyn grabbed a fistful of wire wool and began scrubbing at Thatcher's face with some venom.

"I've always wanted to do this, you villainous old cow! This is for The Valleys! This is for the steel works! This is for the miner's strike! On your way! Be gone!" Glyn cackled loudly as he scrubbed. Kevin still wasn't convinced, but helped his pal by stirring up the whitewash and breaking the crust off the end of his big broad paintbrush. Once the last trace of spray paint was finally ground off the side of the old barn, Glyn grabbed the brush and daubed whitewash coarsely over the spot where the graffiti had been.

"You know what I think about Banksy, Kevin?"

"What's that, Glyn?"

"Bugger Banksy! Bugger him for his smug artsy ways, and for floating in and fucking up people's lives by painting some old shit on the side of their house, without a care for all the bollocks that they'll have to put up with afterwards! Get a real job, mate, rather than just poncing about being clever on purpose all the time!"

And with that, Glyn climbed down from the side of the barn, gathered together all of his decorating materials and let out a big, happy sigh.

"Thank fuck that's gone now, Kevin lad. Now we can just get back to being two stoned morons up the end of a long dark lane!"

"Very good point, Glyn. Very good point."

"Right then, let's leave that to dry for a couple of hours, then we'll have that scaffolding down, and then nobody will be any the wiser to what's been going on up here. I bloody hope!"

The two friends then slowly walked up the steps to the cottage, went in through the door, and put the kettle on.

30

It had been two days now since Glyn had removed every trace of the Banksy from the end of his old barn wall. Sure enough, there had still been a few more visitors up the lane than usual, but most of them had just been studenty types from out of town on a speculative graffiti hunt. Although there was one lost looking father and son pairing with London accents and matching baseball caps that Glyn seriously suspected to be that Team Robbo mob. But now the dread artefact had been removed there was nothing really left to worry about, and Glyn figured that once word got around that the unfinished artwork was most definitely and definitively not up this particular lane, then that steady trickle would soon begin to peter out to the one or two odd drips every now and again. And it had been a relaxing couple of days for Glyn and Kevin, too. Not only did they no longer have to keep an eye out to see what kind of arch nonsense was making its way up their lane, but seeing as they'd sold off all their stock to Bob's brother-in-law, they didn't have to worry about tending the plants day and night, either. They had just enough for their own personal use to tide them over until they needed to start growing it all from seed again, but just for now they were enjoying the little bit of piece and quiet that they'd been given, and felt in no rush to get any other plans and schemes on the go for a while. All they needed to do until the nights started drawing in was to go and sort out the sheep and check the gates every couple of days, make sure that the vegetable patch was fed and watered, and eat biscuits. A lot of biscuits.

It even went surprisingly well with the council when they turned up unannounced that morning. They inspected the barn, from top to bottom, and seemed pleasantly surprised with how well it had been preserved. In fact they even praised Glyn for his constant running repairs of the building.

"We can see how well-looked after it is," said Ros Llewellyn – the council planning officer who accompanied the listing inspector – at the end of her visit, "and were particularly impressed with not only the historic integrity of the building, considering that it's been constantly used on a working farm, but also the lengths to which you've gone to keep it well-painted and to keep the roof space intact. We therefore recommend that this building has full listing status, which will also entitle you to substantial grants for its upkeep, should you indeed need any."

Glyn and Kevin gave each other a sly, conspiratorial smile at this point in the conversation, knowing full well that if the inspectors had visited only a few days earlier it might have been an entirely different story. Just before she left, Miss Llewellyn leaned quietly towards the two fellas and whispered: "You don't happen to know where than Banksy is though, do you now? Nobody seems to know anything about it, and I reckon a couple of young fellas like you might have heard something on the grapevine."

"Nothing concrete," said Kevin, again lying maybe just a little bit, "but I did hear that it might be down in Crosskeys."

Glyn smirked involuntarily at his pal's continued spinning of this yarn, even now it was no longer entirely necessary. But he still did his best for it not to become a terribly obvious smirk.

"Ooh, that might be useful information, Kevin," said Miss Llewellyn. "That's towards the end of our journey, as we started at the top of the valley and we're working our way down. But I can't imagine they'd do anything stupid, like tearing it out of the wall and selling it or anything. We'd be sure to notice that kind of behaviour if they did."

"Oh, and Miss Llewellyn," Kevin asked cheekily, just as the party from the council was leaving, "if you do happen to find this Banksy thing, could you give us a shout, because we'd just love to see it!"

Glyn was now biting his lip trying not to laugh out loud.

"Right you are lads! We will!" Miss Llewellyn sang out of her council company car window, "and again, good work on keeping that lovely old barn in such tremendous condition! Byeeee!"

And with that she sped off, with the lads resisting the urge to roll about in fits of laugher until the car was well out of hearing range.

What made it an even better morning was that old Bob from the Green Dragon was true to his word, and delivered Glyn his down payment of sixteen grand pretty much at the crack of dawn, after he'd told Elaine that he was popping off to his suppliers in Neath to talk about getting some more exotic meats in.

"Lay off that crocodile this time though, Bob," she told him before he left. "Because everyone told me that it was fucking rank!"

While he was at Daisy Farm, though Bob did however let slip that it was him that told the cub reporter from the Gazette about the Banksy on their barn.

"You know what I'm like under pressure, lads," the landlord

flustered. "She asked me straight and I just kind of mumbled it out. It was well before we made the deal about all your garden produce, though. I'll bet you're glad that bloody painting's gone now then!"

"More than you could ever imagine," Glyn told him, a little bit miffed at Bob's latest admission, but seeing as the offending article had now been extinguished from history he thought it more gracious to let it go.

So now, rather than fretting and making furious schemes on how to avoid detection – and perhaps even worse – the two lads were sat out on deckchairs on the little patch of lawn in front of the cottage on a lazy, sunny, late-Autumn Wednesday afternoon, each with a can of cheap Polish beer wedged between their knees and reviewing the ludicrous situation that they'd briefly, but painfully, found themselves in.

"In years to come," said Kevin, "we'll be telling our grandchildren all about this little adventure of ours that we've been having over the last week and a bit, and they won't believe a bloody word of it!"

"Grandchildren!" Glyn scoffed. "We'd have to have bloody children, first, Kevin butt! And before that we'd obviously have to have, you know, girlfriends and that!"

He laughed heartily for a few moments, before quieting a bit, and asking his pal: "How's it going with you and that Summer, mind?"

Kevin looked resigned to his fate.

"Oh I think that ship's long since sailed, Glyn mate. I reckon she only wanted me for my access to the glamour of show business. How terribly fickle of her, eh!"

"Ha, yeah," Glyn laughed. "One sniff of celebrity and they were all hanging round you like a gaggle of footballers wives, butt!"

"Oh no, I don't blame her, Glyn," said Kevin, defending the object of his affection. "She saw a chance of increasing her standing with the tourist information office and she grasped it with both hands. It must be bloody hard trying to run an operation like that around these parts, so a girl had to do what she had to do, isn't it."

"Grasped it with both hands, did she?" Glyn asked, with a dirty laugh on his lips. "Lucky Kevin! Ha! Lucky Summer, even!"

"Oh stop being a smutty twat, Glyn," Kevin grumbled. "It doesn't suit you."

Suddenly the boys' attention was distracted by a quiet rumbling coming from down the lane and the distant voice of a man singing.

"I reckon that's Postman Pete coming with our little package from Banksy, Kevin butt," Glyn said, excitedly. And sure enough, it was.

Postman Pete was a mixed race lad of about the same age as Glyn. His dad was from Trindad, and his Mam from Abertillery, but they'd met at some club in Cardiff in the eighties. It was a proper touching love story, and Pete's dad immediately moved up to live with his new bride in the valley. Not long after, they had Pete. It was obviously a bit tricky at first back then, being one of the only black kids in the school, but he got round it by just being an altogether nice lad, and quickly the teasing and unabashed racism stopped and he became one of the most popular kids in the neighbourhood. Sadly though, by the time he hit his twenties he started to go down with a disease called vitiligo, which attacks the pigment in the skin, making some patches appear lighter than others. It mostly affected his arms and legs, but Pete, already working for the Post Office by then, got around the mickey-taking of his workmates with his characteristic good cheer by singing a very particular song on his rounds.

"Postman Pete, Postman Pete, Postman Pete and his black and white feet."

It started more as a self-defence mechanism, to get the first laugh in himself before anyone else could mock him too much for it, but he still occasionally sung it in comic self-deprecation when he was delivering to the people that he felt most at home with. Somewhat prophetically he ended up marrying a local girl called Jess, so he put up a wooden sign bearing the name 'Greendale' on a sign above the door of his house, just to add to the running joke.

Glyn and Kevin were among his favourite deliveries, so as soon as he got within obvious earshot he began to sing his signature song.

"How's it going, Pete?" Glyn shouted down the lane. "Long time no see!"

"Well I only tend to come up here for bills and postcards these days, Glyn," Pete replied. "I'm fine, butt – how are you two keeping? I heard you had a bit of commotion up here."

Glyn and Kevin explained the whole long and involved story, as Pete sat perched on the frame of his bike, absolutely drawn into the yarn.

"So you've seen this Banksy bloke's face, then?" Pete enquired, excitedly. "Was it anyone you recognised?"

"Nah Pete, just a random looking bloke with a Bristol accent," Kevin replied.

"Ooh, good. That sits in with my theory perfectly," said Pete excitedly.

"What theory's that, Pete?" Glyn asked.

"Well I read a long time ago, in some newspaper or magazine or something," Pete explained, "that it was just some random Bristol geezer called Robin. You know, not one of these pop stars or artists that people keep claiming he is. Just a normal bloke with an eye for graffiti."

"Well it could have been him, I suppose," Glyn answered. "He did just look like a normal bloke. But if his name's Robin, why do they call him Banksy then?"

"Well," said Pete, with a professorial look on his face, "that's where my theory comes in. I wondered for years myself how some bloke called Robin ended up with the name Banksy, and then it dawned on me. Robin. Banks. You know, as in robbing banks. He'd given himself this big up gangsta street name when he started out, then in time it had slowly been shortened to Banksy!"

"Well that's as good a theory as I've ever heard," said Kevin. "I wonder what the real true story is?"

"Oh I'm sure that he'll either be nicked on the job or get stitched up by Panorama some time soon, Kev," said Pete.

"Either that, or he'll start craving the attention and out himself live on The One Show or something," laughed Glyn.

"Ha, imagine that!" Pete laughed. "After all this time he'll appear on live telly, peel back the balaclava, and its Gyles bloody Brandreth!"

"Hiding in plain sight all this time!" Glyn added.

"Anyway lads," said Pete, with a slight gear change, "I'd better get on. I've got a package for you. And it's got some good stamps on it!"

Glyn and Kevin looked at each other in excitement. Could this be the package from that Banksy lad that they'd been expecting?

Pete delved into his sack and fished it out. Sure enough, the stamps weren't from around these parts. There were about a dozen small perforated squares, all stuck on roughly in a big clump in the top right-hand corner of the parcel. Each of them pictured a small cartoon rat and some Chinese writing, with the words 'La Poste' down one side.

"I think they're French, Glyn," Kevin said with a puzzled look on his face. "Who do we know in France?"

"I can't say that I know anybody, Kev," Glyn answered, "And there's no forwarding address apart from a PO Box in London. How very strange!"

"Well go on then, open it!" Pete shouted in mock frustration. "I haven't got all day to stand around here like a lemon!"

"You know that we're expecting a package from Banksy, right Pete," Kevin explained.

"I didn't, but I'm not budging until I find out what's in there now!" Pete replied.

The three men just stood and stared at the parcel for a moment as it rested in Glyn's hands. It was just over a foot long and about eight inches wide. It was wrapped in brown paper and packing tape, but there was clearly a more sturdy box inside, and when Glyn wobbled it gently he could feel that there was something fairly large, with a bit of weight behind it inside.

"Gwan man!" said Pete, now genuinely a bit frustrated, "Get in there my son!"

Glyn picked at a corner of the paper and carefully unwrapped it. Inside was a plain brown cardboard box, fastened with a short piece of clear tape at one end. Glyn ripped off the tape, opened the flap at the end of the box, and slid the contents out. As he pulled it from the cardboard sheath, he slowly revealed a further box, only this one was more solid, and covered in a blue velveteen substance, all held shut with a small brass-coloured metal latch. As he got it fully out of its wrappings, Glyn realised that he'd been holding the box upside down, so turned it over to reveal the familiar Banksy signature tag monogrammed in the centre of the box's lid in shiny gold lettering. The three men drew closer to the mystery package as Glyn paused for a moment.

"What do you think that it's going to be?" Glyn asked his two associates. "Some kind of little statue or something? Or maybe one of his awards for that film he did?"

"Well we're not going to find out until you open it, are we Glyn!" said Pete, now beside himself with anticipation.

Glyn carefully unhitched the latch and slowly opened the box.

"Oh!" he said curtly. "Is that it?"

"What, Glyn, what?" said Kevin excitedly as he'd found himself on the wrong side of the box's lid.

Pete let out a hearty roar of laughter. "It's only a bloody spray can, isn't it, Kevin!"

"You what, Pete?" Kevin asked in some disappointment. "Let's have a look at it."

He moved around the box to get a better view. "Oh yeah, you're right mate. That's a bit of a let down... But hang on a minute what's that bit of paper under the can?"

Glyn's hand darted to pull out the piece of parchment from beneath the can.

"It's a letter, Kev, it's a letter!" he said, the pregnant excitement around the box now ramping up a little more.

"So what does it say, Glyn, what does it say," Pete asked.

"Right then, ahem…" Glyn coughed, as he prepared to read out the note.

"Dear Glyn and Kevin,

I'm so sorry for all the unnecessary aggro that I've caused you these last few days. I never really stopped to realise what a pain in the arse it must be having one of my pieces on your wall before. I always considered them to be something of a rare treat, rather than the utter burden they so often seem to become. To please accept this token of my gratitude and apology. It's the can that I used when I began to spray that terrible Thatcher thing on your wall. There are, to the best of my knowledge, no other unfinished works of mine left on a wall anywhere else in the world, so your painting, together with the stencil and this can, could help it raise a pretty penny at auction some day. I've even signed the can so that nobody can say you've just got it off some skip and you're chancing your luck.

Again, I can only apologise for making your life a misery, and I promise to think more carefully about where I put my works from this day forth.

Your friend,

Banksy

PS Great pitchfork work, Glyn!"

The three men leaned back from the letter for a moment and all pondered the meaning of art for a bit, until Kevin piped up, with a slight hint of sarcasm in his voice.

"So you know what you've done here, Glyn," he slowly announced. "You've defaced a unique and quite possibly priceless work of art with some wire wool and a quick splash of whitewash. You've robbed the nation – nay, the world – of one of art's true treasures. You're no better than that bloke who slashed the Mona Lisa, or that fella that chucked the paint over that pile of bricks in the Tate. No, it's worse, you are no better than the Team Robbo Hit Squad! In fact you're exactly the same. I'll give them a shout – maybe you can get a club card and a t-shirt for joining or something.

Kevin broke character and was now laughing along with the other two.

"Still, it was only a picture of Thatcher having a shit down a coalmine, wasn't it, Kevin," Glyn laughed. "I can't see that having sat on the plush walls of the Prado alongside all the El Grecos and the fine Flemish Masters."

Glyn stopped suddenly and began to look incredibly serious.

"Shit!" he proclaimed.

"What is it?" both Kevin and Pete said as one.

"The stencil!" Glyn replied. "The fucking stencil. We binned the fucking stencil, and here's Banksy telling us that it could be worth something. Oh bloody hell Kevin, what have we done now?"

Pete chipped in with an unexpected question.

"Where did you bin it lads?"

"That skip down the end of our lane. All us lane dwellers drop their old rubbish down there," Glyn answered, gravely.

"Well I'll tell you what, lads, I've just been down by there, and it was absolutely overflowing with tat," Pete told them.

"Actually," Kevin added, "Pete's got a very good point, Glyn. The gate down the bottom of the lane's been locked shut for the best part of a week, and you know how lazy the bastard binmen are around here. They'd never be bothered walking all that way up the lane to grab our wheely skip. And even if they did, they'd leave the empty down by the gate."

"Shit! I think you're actually right there, Kev butt," said Glyn, now looking less anguished. "I reckon it must still be in there somewhere! Let's get down to that bin and fish it out before anything too horrible gets chucked on it!"

And with that, the two friends turned on their heels and pegged it down the lane, with Postman Pete hammering along on his bike behind them. When they got to the big wheeled council bin, they could see that it was overflowing with household waste, but there wasn't anything remotely resembling a stencil in sight.

"There's only one thing for it, Kevin lad," Glyn announced. "Jump in then!"

"I'm not getting in there, Glyn mun!" said Kevin defensively. "There's no way of knowing what Jack and Gary and all them nut jobs further up the lane might have been putting in there! No, let's tip it out! We can always chuck it all back in afterwards."

"Good point, Kev. Get on a corner," said Glyn. "Pete, do you want to help?"

"Can't mate. Still on my round, innit. Can't be getting the uniform dirty," the postman smiled. "I'll watch though!"

"Yeah, cheers mate!" Glyn smiled. "Right, come on Kev, let's push this thing over."

Glyn and Kevin got hold of a corner each and began to push. It was a little tricky at first, but they soon gained momentum, and it crashed to the ground, spewing out a cascade of old beer cans, potato peelings and strangely shaped bits of wood, which were probably leftovers from old Jack's beehives.

"Can you see anything, Kev," said Glyn, urging his pal to climb inside.

"Not yet, Glyn, mate. It's mostly the usual old bin rubbish. Wait, I can see something!"

"What's that Kevin, mate?" Glyn asked.

"I think it's another one of those spray cans that we bunged in here with the stencil," Kevin replied.

"I must almost be on the right strata."

"You're not an bloody archeologist, Kevin mate," laughed Glyn, "You're rooting around in a bloody skip!"

"Yeah," Pete added. "It's not Time Team, it's bloody Tin Team!"

"Oh shut up you two!" Kevin barked back. "And how come I always end up being the one who does all the dirtiest, most gloop encrusted jobs, anyway?"

"I reckon you just gravitate towards them, Kev," said Glyn.

"Yeah, and you evaporate away from them," Kevin grumbled. "Ooh, wait a minute, what's this?"

"What?" asked Glyn.

"This? It's a big bit of thin but firm card, with some tape around the edges and some spray paint on it," came the voice from deep within the bowels of the bin.

"You sure it's not just some of Jack Evans's craft leftovers, Kev," Glyn asked.

"Not sure Glyn," Kevin replied. "I've have a delve a bit further in…"

"Now if you'd have told me that I would end up having this kind of adventure when I started out on my round this morning," laughed Pete, "I'd have righteously laughed in your face! Who'd have thought it, eh!"

"I know, Pete, I know," said Glyn. "Welcome to my week!"

"I think this is it, Glyn," Kevin shouted excitedly. "I'm just pulling it out."

"Careful though, Kevin mun," Glyn suggested. "This is a near priceless artefact, remember. Don't tear its fragile edges."

"I won't, mun, I won't"

There was a bit more rattling about from inside the bin, and a fair bit of frustrated swearing, but eventually Kevin scuttled out like a startled hermit crab, and held the stencil up to the sky. Sure enough, there was Thatcher's strained face pumping whatever the heck it was into the mineshaft from her bowel.

"I mean, it's alright," said Pete, screwing his eyes up to work out what the stencil portrayed, "but it's hardly one of his better works, is it now Glyn."

"You can see why I wanted shot of it off the side of my old barn now, can't you Pete!" said Glyn.

"Oh totally, Glyn. Totally. Right, I'm back off on the rest of my round now," said the postman. "If I see anything to beat this over the next few days I'll be highly surprised!"

"Right cheers then Pete!" Glyn said as the postman climbed back on his bike. "And thanks for all the help!"

"What help did he actually give, Glyn?" said Kevin as he unpeeled an old teabag from the side of his face and brushed some damp wood shavings out of his hair with his grubby fingers. "He just sat on his bike and took the piss!"

"Morale, Kevin. Morale!" Glyn laughed.

"That's easy for you to say, Glyn. You weren't the one up to your neck in old chip wrappers! How do I let you talk me into these things?"

"Right then, let's get back up to the house to get you cleaned up and work out exactly what we're going to do with this bloody rotten old bit of cardboard," said Glyn.

"You know what, Glyn," said Kevin. "I reckon I'm beginning to get a bit of an idea…"

31

"I tell you, Kevin," Glyn said, earnestly. "This could very easily be the very best of all your ideas."

"If it works, Glyn, it's going to be bloody hilarious!" Kevin replied, laughing heartily.

What Kevin had planned was this. Because most of the hard work and dismay from the last week or so was almost entirely down to Bob, the landlord of The Green Dragon, being totally unable to keep his flappy jaws shut, Kevin reckoned that he and Glyn should give him a little surprise of his own and see how much he liked it. And this is what they were going to do…

Under the hours of deep darkness, probably about 3am when all but the most hardy stoners on a biscuit quest were sound asleep, they'd sneak down into Abertillery, tape that bloody horrible stencil onto the big white wall on the side of Bob's pub, get the spray can that Banksy had sent them, and give Bob his own piece of internationally famous art to contend with – along with all the attendant stress and headache that went along with it. Kevin was well aware that they weren't going to be able to offer Banksy's deft touch with a spray can, and that anyone who knew a thing or two about street art would be able to automatically tell that it was a fake. But the fact that they were using an original stencil, cut by the hand of the lad himself, and in the exact colour and make of spray paint that he traditionally uses to make his works, should fox enough people around these parts for just about long enough to exact some manner of comedy revenge on the errant landlord. After all, he couldn't tell the difference from a Banksy and a Breughel, let alone distinguish the deft touch of a master craftsman from that of a couple of goonish chancers having a laugh. The plan was practically perfect in every way, and what with it being in such a highly visible location rather than the out-of-the-way back lane that the original, genuine painting was situated, the word would pretty quickly spread, and he'd have all sorts of people popping round for a look and wanting to get a piece of an action. Kevin had even knocked up a fake Instagram account that looked quite a bit like that of the actual Banksy's, and would be sure to tag the artist's name in the posting of any picture that he would post after they'd completed it, just to be sure that the news would spread even quicker and further.

The two lads gathered together all of the necessary art materials into a big holdall, including a few extra tins of paint that they'd fished out of the bin down the lane just in case they ran out too early.

Then they each hooked a ladder over their right shoulders and began to work their way into town. It was just shy of a two mile trip, door to door, but it absolutely flew by as the lads suppressed giggles and guffaws all the way down, and tried to impersonate what Bob's face might look like when he saw what had appeared on the side of his hostelry.

"First up, he'll have steam coming out of his ears thinking that some local scrote has vandalised his pub wall" suggested Kevin. "Then he'll go through a reasoning stage where he wonders whether this might actually be something of merit, then the pound note signs will start flashing in his eyes like some old fifties cash register when he reckons he's got a Banksy on his side wall!"

Kevin acted out each of these faces one by one as the pair passed Cwmtillery Colliery wheel, and they tried not to laugh too loudly in case they disturbed the neighbours. Glyn, however, had a different idea.

"He's just going to see it, shit his pants, and then pass out there and then when all the options flowing through his nut overload his old brain," he said. "But whatever ends up happening, it'll be bloody delicious, I can tell you now!"

As they got nearer to Abertillery town centre, the two lads got more into stealth mode, keeping as quiet as they could, and doing those little waves and pointy gestures that commandos always do on the telly when they're on some deadly operation – only these boys were doing it each time they had to cross a road or walk round a corner onto a new street. They also kept a reasonable, sensible distance apart so that it wouldn't get too slapstick, because if their ladders were constantly bashing into each other it would make a right old racket.

They finally made it to the pub, then carefully leant each ladder against the pub wall a few feet apart, taking great lengths not to make any kind of rattling at all. Elaine was famously a light sleeper, although that may have had something to do with Bob's snoring, which could sound like a broken hydroelectric turbine on a good night. They each took a corner of the stencil, which they'd sensibly pre-taped, and climbed their ladders in unison, placing the large piece of thin card just high enough so that Bob wouldn't easily be able to attack it with a scrubbing brush. They then smoothed the sticky paper tape to the wall, and added a few more bits to each corner, just to be extra secure, before climbing back down the ladders, again in unison, to fetch the spray can.

"I reckon this is a job for you here, Glyn," Kevin suggested in a whisper. "The original was on your wall, after all, so it would make this whole silly adventure all the more sweet!"

"Right you are, Kev!" Glyn agreed. Quietly. "Now, you foot the ladder and I'll be up there quick as."

Glyn pulled the precious autographed can from a small fabric tote bag and began to spray, furiously. He reckoned that he'd filled every gap in the cardboard, so got down off the ladder just to check. He hadn't. He'd managed to miss out a couple of the corners that were the furthest to reach, and a big chunk in the middle of Thatcher's body. So he gently moved his ladder to a better position, coloured in the missing sections, and stood back to admire his work.

"It doesn't need to be too perfect, mind Glyn," said Kevin. "That way it'll be all the funnier when it turns out to be an obvious fake."

"Good point Kev," said Glyn. "I'll pack up now."

As the two lads peeled away the stencil, they could see the beautiful, ugly mark that remained on the side of the wall. When the whole thing was painted in full it was clear what it was supposed to be. There was the stylised Thatcher, straining one out down a toilet-shaped pit head. Below her, gently dropping into the pit below, were golden coins. Kevin had fished some old metallic paint out of the back shed to make this bit look more clear and effective. As Banksy himself had said, it wasn't perhaps one of his best, but even this rough hewn version had the immediate signature look and feel of one of his real works, so they were sure that it would trick old Bob into thinking that he was sitting on a literal gold mine for at least a couple of days.

"He's going to go bloody nuts when he finds out it's a fake, Kev," Glyn whispered.

"I know, Glyn butt," Kevin replied, "and I hope I'm in the bloody vicinity when he does!"

The two men quietly packed up their gear and took the long stroll back to Daisy Farm. As they sat there on their respective sofas, clucking out the occasional snort of amusement into their cups of tea, they mused over what they'd just done.

"I'm keeping that spray can and its fancy box, mind," said Glyn. "That'll look lovely on the dresser, and it'll remind us of all this silly nonsense when we're old and grumbly. Well, more grumbly. Makes you wonder what all this bloody art larky is all about, though, doesn't it though Kevin."

"How do you mean, Glyn?"

"Well Kev, we just used a stencil, created by Banksy, to spray exactly the same can of paint that Banksy would have used, on a random wall in The Valleys, and what we just put up there isn't going to be worth the paint stripper it's going to take to wipe the thing off. But if the lad himself had done it it could be worth thousands. No, millions! Is it all entirely down to whose finger is on the nozzle, Kev? It can't be as simple as that, surely?"

"Well it is a bit. But don't forget, Glyn. He had the idea, designed the original drawings, cut out the stencil with his own hands, worked out where he was going to put it, and then put his well-trained finger on the nozzle and sprayed with a bit more subtlety than either of us ham-fisted buggers could have ever have managed," explained Kevin. "And what's more, he usually puts in some final highlighting detail in a different colour, either freehand or by using another stencil. If either of us had tried that it would have looked like that painting of Jesus in that church in Italy after that old Nan had had a go at restoring it."

"Ha, very good point, Kevin, and excellently made," said Glyn, nodding at his friend's art knowledge.

"It's like that bloke who done that pile of bricks in the seventies that I was talking about earlier, Glyn…" Kevin continued.

"Oh I remember that," Glyn cut in. "Bag of shite that was. Even I could have done that!"

"Yeah, but that's the point, Glyn. You didn't. None of us did. Only some clever sod who had the connections and the training and knew that it would cause a bit of a stir."

"I'll never get my head around it all, Kevin," said Glyn with a confused look on his face. "But does this still mean that this stencil we've just fished out of the bin might actually be worth something? I mean, underneath all my dolloping it's got some paint that Banksy himself has most definitely sprayed on himself – with his cultured finger and all. And he's designed it and cut it out with his own scissors, no doubt?"

"I reckon we might get a few grand for it, Glyn mun," Kevin reasoned. "I wonder who we know who can help us get a buyer for it?"

"Well that André bloke seemed like a bit of a snake oil salesman, didn't he," Glyn said. "I'm not entirely sure that he'd give us the best price for it. That Waldemar laddie said as much, too. In fact, I'm sure that Waldemar will know how exactly to help us. Fetch us that card of his off the mantle, Kev butt – I'll give him a ring in the morning."

ABOUT ROY D HACKSAW

For a council house kid from the middle of nowhere in the early eighties, the only real method of expressing yourself after leaving school was to shout very loud and bash things in a punk rock band. After stints in the nearly successful outfits DATWMF, the Beach Bums and the Cesspit Rebels, Roy remembered that an old English teacher told him he could write a bit and started up the fanzine Xerox Heaven, which was mostly about other fanzines. From there on he stumbled about doing the occasional writing gig before he found himself in London at the turn of the century editing an early student lifestyle website for Jim Kerr out of Simple Minds. That's when he realised that he could probably start doing this larky for a living. Since then his journalistic highlights have included reviewing a noise festival in Shanghai for Metal Hammer, reporting from every Eurovision Song Contest since 1998, and answering the readers' letters in Disney Princess magazine in the voice of Jessie The Cowgirl from Toy Story.

More recently he's turned his hand to documentary filmmaking, and his first short film, The Bard's Wife, was nominated for a dozen awards at festivals worldwide, and won a runners-up gong in the Whicker's World Foundation Awards at the Sheffield Doc/Fest in 2017.

On top of that, he's a retired semi-professional game show contestant, having appeared on shows as varied as The Weakest Link and Fifteen To One, via The Chase and Total Wipeout, to University Challenge and Mastermind, where his specialist subject was the children's TV series Trumpton. In a case of poacher-turned-gamekeeper he now writes the questions, most notably on Tipping Point where he became the most prolific writer in the show's history.

But he's still happiest when he's making a right old racket on stage in a dirty pub front of a handful of people, and is currently a member of the veteran bogroll-chucking duo Hacksaw, Bristol noise rock merchants GlueHorse, and the newly reformed eighties punk legends Chaotic Dischord.

He has absolutely no idea how he keeps getting away with all this nonsense, and fully expects to get found out for the chancer he is any day soon.

Roy was inspired to write Bugger Banksy after the illusive artist chucked up an artwork opposite his local chippy for Valentine's Day, and he watched the unwelcome chaos that ensued for the unfortunate souls that lived on the other side of the wall.

Roy D Hacksaw
Writer, filmmaker, punk rock singer